Dear Reader:

Welcome to my world of L.A. CONNECTIONS. I have been toying with the idea for some time of writing a serial novel, and last year when I wrote a special four-part series for *TV Guide,* and received so many of your wonderful letters, I knew that I wanted to make it bigger and better! L.A. CONNECTIONS is a story about a high-profile murder in Los Angeles. This four-part novel brings together a group of diverse characters—true life people, cleverly disguised, that I have observed in all the years I have lived in Hollywood. My heroine, Madison Castelli, is just the kind of woman I like writing about best—strong, feisty, independent. She is a journalist who comes to L.A. on assignment from the magazine *Manhattan Style.* They want her to cover the life of superagent Freddie Leon—a man with enormous power and his own devious agenda.

I know many of you loved the character of Lucky Santangelo, a heroine I created in four of my books: *Chances, Lucky, Lady Boss,* and *Vendetta: Lucky's Revenge.* With Madison, I have tried to create a character just as charismatic.

Writing is my passion, and bringing a serial novel to life is a wonderful challenge. First comes *Power,* followed by *Obsession,* then *Murder,* and finally, *Revenge.*

When you read something that really grabs your attention, it should be a great visual trip so that you can imagine the characters. In all my seventeen books, I feel I've captured the essence of the lives I have observed. Of course, I've changed the names to protect the not-so-innocent!

Writing L.A. CONNECTIONS was an adventure. I hope you join me for all four parts, and that it will keep you reading way into the night.

Stay with me—I promise you we'll have fun!

Happy Reading,

Books by Jackie Collins

Thrill!
Vendetta: Lucky's Revenge
Hollywood Kids
American Star
Lady Boss
Rock Star
Hollywood Husbands
Lucky
Hollywood Wives
Chances
Lovers and Gamblers
The World Is Full of Divorced Women
The Love Killers
Sinners
The Bitch
The Stud
The World Is Full of Married Men

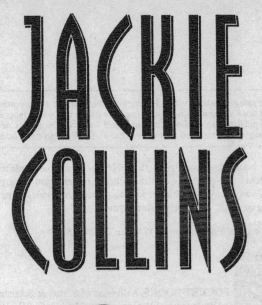

JACKIE COLLINS

Power

POCKET BOOKS
New York   London   Toronto   Sydney   Tokyo   Singapore

This book is a work of fiction. Names, characters, places and incidents are products of the author's imagination or are used fictitiously. Any resemblance to actual events or locales or persons, living or dead, is entirely coincidental.

An *Original* Publication of POCKET BOOKS

POCKET BOOKS, a division of Simon & Schuster Inc.
1230 Avenue of the Americas, New York, NY 10020

Copyright © 1998 by Chances, Inc.

ISBN: 0-671-02458-2

First Pocket Books printing September 1998

10 9 8 7 6 5 4 3 2 1

POCKET and colophon are registered trademarks of Simon & Schuster Inc.

Back cover photo by Greg Gorman

Printed in the U.S.A.

Prologue

Los Angeles
1997

IT WAS NEAR MIDNIGHT when the gleaming blue Mercedes limousine pulled up outside the closed book store in Farmer's Market, on Fairfax. A uniformed chauffeur—dressed all in black, including leather gloves and impenetrable sunglasses—stepped out of the car and glanced around.

Nearby, a pretty girl sitting in her parked Camaro hurriedly said goodbye to her girlfriend, with whom she had been chatting on her cell phone, and left her car, locking it behind her.

"Hi," she said, approaching the weird-looking chauffeur. "I'm Kimberly. Are you here for Mister X?"

He nodded and opened the rear door for her. She

3

climbed in. He closed the door and got in the front seat.

"Mister X requires you to put on a blindfold," he said without turning around. "You will find it on the seat beside you."

Okay, Kimberly thought. *A kinky one. But that's nothing new.* Kimberly (real name Mary Ann Jones, formerly of Detroit) had been a Hollywood call girl for eighteen months, and during that time she'd seen plenty. Wearing a blindfold in the back of a limousine was nothing compared to some of the things she'd been asked to do.

She put on the soft velvet blindfold and settled back, almost falling asleep as the limo sped to its destination.

Twenty minutes later the car slowed, and she heard the clanking sound of heavy gates opening.

"Can I take the blindfold off now?" she asked, leaning forward.

"Kindly wait," the chauffeur replied.

A few moments later the limo pulled to a stop. Kimberly adjusted her dress, a skimpy designer number she'd picked up at Barney's warehouse sale. Then she fluffed out her hair, blond and curly.

The chauffeur opened the door. "Get out," he commanded.

She removed the blindfold without asking, and followed him to the entrance of a large mansion. He opened the door with a key and ushered her inside the dark entry hall.

"Wow!" Kimberly said, squinting at an enormous chandelier hanging above them. "Wouldn't want to be under *that* in an earthquake!"

"Here's your fee," the chauffeur said, handing her an envelope bulging with cash.

She took the envelope and stuffed it in her brown leather shoulder bag—a Coach original she'd purchased in Century City that same day. "Where's Mister X?" she asked. "In the bedroom?"

"No," the chauffeur replied. "Outside."

"Whatever," she said, thrusting out her size-36 C-cup breasts—purchased shortly after she'd first come to Hollywood, on the heels of winning a beauty contest back home.

"Whatever," the chauffeur mimicked, taking her arm and leading her through an ornate living room to French doors that took them out to a black-bottomed swimming pool.

The man had a firm grip on her arm—too firm for her liking. And how dare he mimic her, she thought. Where the hell was Mister X? She was ready to get this over and done with so she could get home to her live-in boyfriend—a sometime male-model-slash-porn-star with muscles of steel.

"Mister X would like to know if you can swim?" the chauffeur said, stopping beside the pool.

"Nope," she replied, wondering why he didn't put on some lights—the place was downright gloomy. "Although I'm thinking of taking lessons."

"You'd better start now," the chauffeur said. And before she was aware of what was happening he had shoved her violently into the deep end of the pool.

She sank to the bottom, rising to the surface seconds later spluttering and choking, her arms flailing wildly in the air. "Help!" she screamed, gasping for air. "I told you—I . . . can't . . . swim."

The chauffeur stood by the edge of the pool, his member out, right hand working hard.

"Help me!" Kimberly yelled, struggling desperately before vanishing under the water for the second time.

The man continued to go about his business, climaxing over the girl's head as she surfaced again.

"You're *crazy!*" she screamed, before going down for the third time.

And after that, everything went black.

One Year Later

chapter 1

MADISON CASTELLI DID not particularly enjoy covering Hollywood stories. Lifestyles of the rich and decadent was not her thing—which is exactly why her editor, Victor Simons, had insisted she was the right person for the assignment. "You're not into all that Hollywood bullshit," he'd said. "You don't want anything from the so-called power elite, which makes you the perfect journalist to get me the real inside story on Mr. Super-Power, Freddie Leon. Besides, you're beautiful, so he'll pay attention."

Ha! Madison thought ruefully as she boarded an American Airlines flight to L.A. *I'm so beautiful that three months ago, David, my live-in love of two years, went out for a pack of cigarettes and never came back.*

What he *did* do was leave her a cowardly note all about how he couldn't deal with commitment and would never be able to make her happy. Five weeks later she'd found out he'd married his childhood sweetheart—a vapid blonde with huge boobs and a serious overbite.

So much for avoiding commitment.

Madison was twenty-nine years old and extremely attractive, although she played her good looks down by wearing functional clothes and barely any makeup. But try as she might, nothing could disguise her almond-shaped eyes, sharply defined cheekbones, seductive lips, smooth olive skin, and black unruly hair she usually wore pulled back in a severe ponytail. Not to mention her lithe, five-foot-eight-inch body, with full breasts, narrow waist and long dancer's legs.

Madison did not consider herself beautiful. Her idea of good looks was her mother, Stella—a statuesque blonde whose dreamy eyes and quivering lips reminded most people of Marilyn Monroe.

Looks-wise, Madison took after her father, Michael, the best-looking fifty-eight-year-old in Connecticut. She'd also inherited his steely determination and undeniable charm—two admirable qualities that had not hindered her rise to success as a well-respected writer of revealing profiles of the rich, notorious and powerful.

Madison loved what she did—going for the right angle, discovering the hidden secrets of people in the public eye. Politicians and super-rich business tycoons were her favorite interviews. Movie stars, sports personalities and Hollywood moguls were low on her list. She didn't regard herself as a killer, although she did write with searing honesty, sometimes upsetting the people she wrote about, who were usually sheltered in an all-enveloping cocoon of protective P.R.

Too bad if they didn't like it; she was merely telling the truth.

Settling into her first-class window seat, she glanced around the cabin, spotting Bo Deacon, a well-known TV host with an equally well-known drug habit. Bo did not look well; puffy-faced and slack-jawed, he still managed to come to life when the cameras rolled on his popular late-night talk show.

Madison hoped that the seat next to her would remain vacant, but it was not to be. At the last moment a breathy, busty blonde in a micro black leather dress was escorted aboard by two starstruck airline reps who practically carried her to her seat. Madison recognized the girl as Salli T. Turner, the current darling of the tabloids. Salli was the star of *Teach!*, a half-hour weekly TV sitcom in which she played a comely swimming teacher who visited a different glamorous mansion every week, causing havoc and saving lives—all the while dressed in a minuscule one-piece black rubber swimsuit, which only served to enhance her pneumatic breasts, twenty-inch waist and endless legs.

"Wow!" Salli exclaimed, collapsing into her seat and fluffing out her mane of blond curls. "Just made it!"

"Are you okay, Miss Turner?" asked anxious airline rep number one.

"What can I get you?" asked overeager airline rep number two.

Both men were bug-eyed, staring down her ample cleavage as if they'd never seen anything like it before. *And they probably haven't,* Madison thought.

"Everything's hunky-dory, guys," Salli said, favoring them with a toothy grin. "My husband's meeting me in L.A. If I'd missed the flight he would've been blue-assed pissed!"

"I can believe *that,*" said airline rep number one, eyes still bugging.

"Me, too!" agreed the other man.

Madison buried her head in *Newsweek*—the last thing she needed was a conversation with this airhead. She vaguely heard the flight attendant asking the men to leave so they could prepare for takeoff; then, shortly after, the big plane began taxiing down the runway.

Without warning, Salli suddenly clutched Madison's arm, causing her to almost drop her magazine.

"I *hate* flying," Salli squeaked, big blue eyes blinking rapidly. "I mean, it's not exactly *flying* I hate, more like *crashing.*"

Carefully Madison prised the girl's fingers off her arm. "Close your eyes, take a deep breath and slowly count to a hundred," she advised. "I'll let you know when we're airborne."

"Gee, thanks," Salli said gratefully. "Didn't think of doing that."

Madison frowned. Clearly this was going to be a long flight. Why couldn't she be stuck next to someone more *interesting?*

She folded her magazine and gazed out of the window as the plane took off. Unlike Salli, she loved flying. The sudden rush of speed, that exhilarating feeling of excitement when the wheels left the ground, the initial ascent—it always gave her a thrill, however many times she'd done it.

Salli sat silently beside her, eyes squeezed tightly shut, pouty lips slowly mouthing numbers.

By the time she opened her eyes they were in the air. "Radical shit!" Salli exclaimed, turning to Madison. "You're *amazing!*"

"Nothing to it," Madison murmured.

"No, *really,*" Salli insisted. "Your advice actually *worked!*"

"I'm glad," Madison said, wishing Miss Rubber Suit (she'd seen the show once—it was titillating trash) would keep her eyes closed for the entire trip.

Rescue arrived in the form of Bo Deacon, who came ambling over holding a glass of Scotch. "Salli, my darling!" he exclaimed. "You look absolutely edible."

"Oh, hi Bo," Salli said guilelessly. "Are you on this plane?"

Smart question, Madison thought wryly. *It's so nice to be traveling with intellectuals.*

"Yeah, honey, I'm sitting over there," he said, gesturing across the aisle. "Got some old bag next to me. Whyn't we try getting her to trade places?"

Salli fluttered her long fake eyelashes. "How are your ratings going?" she asked, as if that would be the deciding factor on whether she changed seats or not.

"Hardly as hot as yours, babe," he leered. "Whyn't I go back and ask the old bag to move?"

"I'm kinda comfortable where I am," Salli said.

"Don't be silly," Bo said. "We *should* sit together, that way we can talk about your next appearance on my show. Last time you were on we got better ratings than Howard."

Salli giggled, pleased with the compliment. "I did Howard's *E!* cable show in New York," she said, small pink tongue licking her jammy lips. "He's *sooo* rude, but cute with it."

"You're the first broad I've heard call Howard Stern cute," Bo said, shaking his head.

"Well, he is," Salli said. "He's kind of big and gangly, and he's always talking about his little dick. *My* guess is he's really got a whopper!"

Madison realized she was actually sitting next to a real live cliché—the definitive Hollywood blonde. If she recounted this exchange to any of her New York friends, they wouldn't believe her.

"You know what?" Madison said, leaning forward, speaking directly to Bo. "If it'll help out, I can change places with you."

Bo noticed her for the first time. "Hey, little lady, that's very sweet of you," he said, putting on his voice that said "I'm a big star, but I can actually be nice to real people."

"Little lady?" Was he kidding?

"On one condition," Salli interrupted.

"What's that, honey?" Bo said.

"I've *got* to sit next to this woman when we land. She's the greatest. She got me through takeoff. She's like some kind of, you know, magical medicine man."

Bo raised an eyebrow. "Really?" he said, taking another look at Madison. "You one of those broads with special powers, honey? Maybe *you* should come on my show."

"Thanks for the offer, Mr. Deacon," Madison answered coolly. "I have a hunch you should stick with Max the chimp."

Bo winked. "So you watch the show, huh?"

When I can't sleep, she wanted to say. *When I've seen every old movie, and Letterman and Leno are in repeats, and I'm absolutely desperate.* "Sometimes," she said, with a pleasant smile, gathering her things, getting up and moving across the aisle to Bo's vacant seat.

The woman he'd referred to as an old bag was an attractive businesswoman in her forties diligently working on her laptop.

"Hi," Madison said. "I'm switching places with Mr. Deacon. Do you mind?"

The woman raised her eyes. "The pleasure is all mine," she said. "I actually thought I'd have to *talk* to him."

They both laughed.

Madison grinned. This was more her kind of traveling partner.

chapter 2

"**I** DON'T GIVE A FUCK," FREDdie Leon said, staring coldly at the short bearded man, who sat uncomfortably in a Biedermeier chair across the other side of Freddie's enormous steel and glass desk.

"I'm telling you, Freddie," the man said, somewhat agitated. "The bitch won't do it."

"Listen," Freddie repeated. "If *I* say she'll do it, it'll happen."

"Then you'd better speak to her."

"I intend to."

"And soon."

"Don't push it, Sam."

Freddie's demeanor was as cold as an Eskimo's dick. He did not appreciate anyone advising him.

He had not become the most powerful superagent in Hollywood by listening to other people, especially a man such as Sam Lowski, a half-assed personal manager whose only real claim to fame was his one big client, Lucinda Bennett—major diva, major pain in the ass, major talent.

Freddie Leon was a poker-faced man of forty-six. He had cordial features, ordinary brown hair, matching eyes and a quick, bland smile which rarely reached his eyes. Head and part owner of the powerful I.A.A.—International Artists Agents— he was nicknamed "the snake" because he could skillfully slither in and out of any deal. Nobody ever dared call him "the snake" to his face. His wife, Diana, had done so once. It was the only time he'd raised his hand to her.

Sam got up to leave. Freddie didn't stop him— he had nothing else to say.

As soon as Sam was out the door, Freddie waited a beat and picked up the phone, speed-dialing Lucinda Bennett's private number. Lucinda answered, sounding sleepy.

"How's my favorite client?" Freddie asked, putting all the charm he could muster into his cold, flat voice.

"Asleep," Lucinda replied grumpily.

"Alone?" Freddie questioned.

An arch laugh. "None of your business."

Freddie cleared his throat. "What's all this I hear about you being a naughty girl?"

"Don't talk down to me, dear," Lucinda said,

her voice languid. "I'm too old and too rich to take that kind of crapola."

"I'm not talking down to you," Freddie replied. "I'm merely reminding you that good behavior always wins in the end."

"I guess Sam crawled in to see you," Lucinda said, the lack of respect she felt for her personal manager coloring her tone.

"Exactly," Freddie replied. "He tells me you're planning on backing out of the Kevin Page movie."

"He's absolutely right."

Freddie checked his irritation. Remaining cool was a requisite of his profession. "Why would you want to do a thing like that when the deal is already in place, and you're getting twelve million dollars?" he asked.

"Because Kevin Page is too young for me," Lucinda responded crisply. "I hardly want to look like an old hag on screen."

"I told you three weeks ago, Lucinda, it's in your contract—they'll hire the cinematographer of your choice. You can look eighteen if you want to."

"I'm almost forty, Freddie," she snapped. "I have no desire to look eighteen."

He knew for a fact she was at least forty-five. "Okay," he said calmly. "Twenty-eight, thirty-eight—whatever age pleases you."

"Don't try to placate me. Kevin Page is your client. He's made two hit movies, and now you think you can cement his career by teaming him with me."

"Not true. This deal is about you. It's essential that you keep reaching that younger audience. Demographics count." He paused before continuing. "You're an enormous star, Lucinda, there's nobody bigger. But you've also got to realize that there're plenty of young people who've never heard of you."

"Screw you, Freddie," she responded furiously. "I can do what I want."

"No," Freddie said, his voice hardening. "You can't. You'll do what *I* say."

"And if I refuse?"

"Then I'll no longer be your agent."

"Freddie, dear, sometimes I think you don't get it," Lucinda said, her icy diva voice piercing his ear. "Agents should be kissing my left toe to represent me."

"If that's what you want, Lucinda," he said, his tone perfectly cool.

"Maybe it is," she said, challenging him.

"Let me know," he said. And then he played his ace card. "Oh, by the way—remember that time way, way back, when you asked me to get hold of some early photographs your first husband took of you, and I was able to do so?"

"Yes."

"Strange thing," he said slowly. "I was going through my safe the other day, and it seems I still have a set of negatives."

Her voice rose, hot with disbelief. "Are you *blackmailing* me, Freddie?"

"No," he said evenly. "Merely trying to get you

to sign a contract which has been on your desk for over a week. A contract that'll pay you twelve million dollars, star you with the hottest young actor in the country, *and* keep your career at the top, exactly where it should be." He paused, allowing her to mull over what he'd said. "Think about it, Lucinda, and let me know before the end of the day." Before she could reply, he replaced the receiver.

Actresses! They'd had to suck so much dick on the way up that once they made it, all they wanted to do was cause trouble.

But nobody caused trouble for Freddie Leon.

He had the power, and he was not shy about using it.

chapter 3

NATALIE DE BARGE CON-
sulted her Bulgari Swatch watch, a recent present
to herself, and swore softly under her breath. How
come time passed so quickly? She was running late
again, and it made her crazy. She had so much to
do before meeting her best friend and old college
roommate, Madison, at the airport. *And,* on top of
everything else, after driving to LAX, she then had
to get back to the studio in time for her spot on the
six-o'clock news, where she was the show-biz news
person on a local TV station. And although she
enjoyed what she did, she certainly aspired to do
more than cover trivial gossip and even more
trivial show-biz events.

Natalie was an extremely vivacious twenty-nine-year-old black woman, with glowing skin, wide brown eyes and a curvaceous body. The bane of her life was the fact that she was only five feet, two inches tall, which really pissed her off, because she would have loved to have been born long and lean like Madison—whom she was genuinely excited about seeing. They spoke at least twice a week, but it wasn't as good as living in the same city. Recently Natalie had split with her out-of-work artist boyfriend, Denzl. Quite convenient, since Madison was no longer with David. Ah yes, Natalie thought, they would certainly have plenty to discuss.

Natalie had already convinced herself that she hardly missed Denzl at all, although he *had* possessed a truly beautiful body. The sad truth was that sometimes a beautiful body was not enough. Denzl had leeched off her for over a year, and when she'd stopped paying the bills, he'd disappeared in the middle of the night with her expensive stereo equipment and entire CD collection of soul classics. She missed Marvin Gaye and Al Green more than she missed him.

"Hey you," said Jimmy Sica, the nighttime news anchor recently hired out of Denver. "What's with the hairstyle?"

Natalie turned, checking Jimmy out. He was six feet tall and extraordinarily handsome, which didn't impress her at all, because she wasn't into perfect good looks—she preferred her men more on the edgy side. "I cut it," she said, casually touching her short, sleek do. "You like?"

"Makes you look about twelve."

She grinned. "Gee, thanks! I *think* that's a compliment in this town."

"Long hair, short hair—you always look great," Jimmy said, smiling. He had a gorgeous smile— and a gorgeous fair-haired wife whose picture he kept prominently displayed on his desk.

"Why, thank you, Jimmy," she said, putting on an exaggerated Southern accent. "I never thought you noticed."

Jimmy flashed his best anchor man smile, revealing perfect teeth and a strong jawline. "All the guys around here notice you."

Was Jimmy Sica coming on to her? No way.

"I'm meeting my girlfriend later," Natalie said, quickly changing the subject. "She's flying in from New York to research a story on Freddie Leon."

Jimmy was suitably impressed. "The agent?"

"Is there another Freddie Leon?"

"Sounds like an interesting gig."

"Madison's an interesting woman."

Jimmy zeroed in for a long lingering look. "If she's *your* friend, I'm sure she is."

"Uh . . . maybe I'll bring her to the studio one day, give her the grand tour."

"I've got a better idea. My wife and I are having a small dinner on Saturday at the house—why don't you bring your friend over? My brother's in town, and a couple of old college buddies. We can make it a party."

"What kind of party did you have in mind, Jimmy?" she asked coyly.

"Not *that* kind of party, honey," he said with a quick laugh. "Sorry to disappoint you, but I'm the straightest guy in town."

"I *know*," she said, mildly flirting in spite of the fact that he wasn't her type. "That's what I like about you."

He raised an expressive eyebrow. "Really?"

"Yes, really."

They exchanged smiles. *Hmm*, she thought, *he's definitely coming on to me*. Which made her slightly uncomfortable because he was married. Besides, he was way too tall for her.

"I'll run it by Madison and let you know," she said.

"Great," he said.

Yeah. Great. Maybe his brother would turn out to be the big love of her life—the prince she was forever searching for. Black, white, multicolored—the right guy had to be out there *somewhere*.

Sure. And John F. Kennedy, Jr., is gay.

"I'm outta here," she said, giving him a little wave. "See you later."

Jimmy Sica smiled his brilliant smile. "You can bet I'll be looking forward to it."

chapter 4

THE PHONE RANG IN KRIStin Carr's pale peach apartment. It was past noon and she was asleep. In a vague fog she heard the loud ringing and waited for Chiew to pick up. To her annoyance, her lazy maid didn't do so.

Hazily Kristin realized it must be her private line. *Shit!* She didn't feel great. Too much Dom Perignon and coke the previous night, and a couple of Halcion to help her sleep. *Shit!*

Her long white arm snaked out from under pale peach satin sheets, groping for the receiver. "Yes?" she murmured, husky-voiced.

"Mister X would like to see you," said a female voice.

"Oh, God, Darlene. Not again! I told you after the last time, I'm not interested."

"Would four thousand cash change your mind?"

"Why me?" she groaned.

"Because you're the best."

Kristin thought about her two previous encounters with Mister X. The first time she'd met him in an underground parking lot in Century City as instructed. He was driving a dark pickup truck with no visible plates and was dressed entirely in black—including opaque sunglasses and a pulled-down baseball cap. Without leaving the truck he'd requested that she strip naked in the parking structure—which fortunately was deserted—and while she circled bare-assed around his truck, he'd jacked off. When he was finished he'd silently handed her an envelope through the window containing two thousand dollars, then hurriedly driven off.

The second time she'd met him in the back row of a movie theater in Westwood at noon. The darkened cinema was deserted, an Eddie Murphy movie played on the big screen, and Mister X was once more in deep disguise. He'd sat next to her, told her to remove her panties and hand them to him, then he'd satisfied himself on the panties and handed them back to her with an envelope containing cash. When she got out of the theater he was long gone.

It was the easiest money she'd ever made and also the weirdest. Mister X gave her a bad feeling.

"He's a freak," she said.

"Force yourself," Darlene said.

"All right," she said grumpily, tempted by the exorbitant amount of money, although her instinct warned her to say no.

"It won't be so bad."

"How do *you* know?"

"It's not as if he beats you up or anything. In fact, you told me that last time he didn't so much as touch you."

"I wish he had," Kristin said heatedly. "Then at least I'd know he was *human.*"

"His money says he's human. That should suffice."

"Okay, okay," Kristin said with a deep sigh. "What dump do I have to meet him at this time?"

"Hollywood Boulevard. A motel past La Brea. I'll fax you the exact address. He wants you there at seven. And wear white—including shoes, hose and sunglasses."

"Does that mean I get a clothes allowance too?" Kristin drawled sarcastically.

"Four thousand's not bad," Darlene pointed out. "That's a thousand up on last time."

"Big fucking deal."

"Have fun."

Darlene's a great madam, Kristin thought bitterly. *All she cares about is the almighty buck. Screw safety.*

She slid out of bed and into the shower. Kristin was the original golden girl—everything natural. A sweep of long blond hair; all-American features; a curvaceous body with large breasts; and a tangle of fluffy gold pubic hair that turned grown men into horny little boys.

She looked like an angel. But she had a heart of stone and a calculator for a brain.

Kristin had a plan. The moment she had accumulated half a million dollars cash in her safe-deposit box, she was out of the business. Every little four thousand dollars helped.

But still . . . Mister X again, the second time in a week. She shuddered at the thought.

Reaching for a soft pink bathrobe, she wrapped it around her glorious body.

Oh, well, another day. Another step toward her goal.

Eventually she'd be free.

chapter 5

"**W**HAT A JERK!" SALLI T. Turner exclaimed, her heavily glossed shell pink lips turning down at the corners, signaling her disapproval.

"Excuse me?" said Madison. She had just settled back into her original seat and was busy thinking about her interview with Freddie Leon—an interview that, if all went smoothly, was due to take place very soon. Victor had promised to set it up through his connection with a mutual friend, even though Freddie Leon was famous for never speaking to the press. In the meantime, Madison planned on talking to his friends, acquaintances, clients and enemies. In fact, anyone who had anything to say about the man.

Salli leaned closer, allowing Madison a frighten-ing close-up of her mascara-caked false lashes. *She's too pretty for that much makeup,* Madison thought. *Why doesn't someone tell her?*

"Bo," Salli said in a half whisper. "He's a real horny asshole."

"I, uh . . . don't know him," Madison said, won-dering why Salli had decided to confide in her.

"You don't have to," Salli snorted derisively. "He's a man, isn't he? And a famous one at that." She wrinkled her snub nose. "All these famous guys think they can get anyone. Do you *know* what he asked me to do?"

"What?" Madison asked, her natural curiosity aroused.

"Invited me into the john so we could make out," Salli whispered. "Only he didn't put it that politely."

"Are you serious?"

"Girl Scout's honor," Salli said. "Ha! Like I'd do it with *him* again. I mean, just 'cause I've got big boobs, blond hair and the whole bimbo bit, men think I'm like *hanging* around, *waiting* for 'em."

"It must be a problem," Madison murmured sympathetically, wondering what Salli meant by "again."

"I can handle it," Salli said, summoning up attitude. "In fact, I get off on the attention." She shrugged, tugging at her short leather skirt. "Hey—I know I have the equipment, but it's not like I'm *dumb* or anything."

"I'm sure you're not," Madison said gently.

"No, I mean *really,*" Salli said, becoming quite heated. "I've used what I've got to get where I am today 'cause it's the only way I could get noticed. Clint Eastwood used what *he* had to become a star. We're just different, that's all."

Madison didn't think it was prudent to point out that Clint Eastwood had been in the business for over thirty years, and had produced and directed many movies. Plus he had his own company and an impeccable professional reputation. But who knew? Maybe thirty years down the line Salli would have the same—stranger things had happened.

"Here's the truth," Salli said, leaning even closer, so that Madison could smell her peppermint-tinged breath. "My boobs are silicone, 'cause I *know* big boobs turn guys on. I've had all the fat sucked out of my thighs, and some of it pumped back into my lips. I bleach my hair and wear sexy clothes. I'm the proof that it all works. It got me a TV series and a *sensational* husband. *Wait* till you meet Bobby, he'll be at the airport."

"I'd like to," Madison said.

"He's a stud!" Salli boasted. "He'd *kill* Bo Deacon if he heard how disrespectful he was to me."

"Then I suggest you don't tell him."

Salli widened her eyes. "I'm not *stupid.*"

"Did you know Bo before?" Madison asked.

"A long time ago . . . before I made it," Salli said. "Then after I got famous, I was on his show a few times and we like *flirted* on camera. Nothing

32

unusual about *that,* I flirt with them all—
Letterman, Leno, Howard. *Everyone* does—
Pamela Anderson, Heather Locklear, even Julia
Roberts. That's the deal. It's expected." She picked
up her drink. "Now I'm *married,* so he shouldn't be
coming on to me. It's not nice."

"You're right," Madison agreed.

"Anyway," Salli continued. "I'm sure you're
bored with hearing all about me. What do *you* do?"

"You'll hate this," Madison said wryly, thinking
that maybe she should have mentioned it before.

"What?"

"I'm a journalist."

Salli burst into peals of girlish laughter. "Oh, no!
A snoop! And here I am spilling the goods. Now I
suppose I'll be all over the cover of the *Star* or the
Enquirer. True confessions of a sex queen. I'm *such*
a ditz!"

"Not *that* kind of journalist," Madison said
quickly. "I write for *Manhattan Style.*"

"Wow!" Salli responded, her big blue eyes full of
surprise. "That's classy stuff. They'd never write
about someone like little old *me.*" A short hopeful
pause. "Would they?"

"Why not? You'd be an interesting interview."

"You think?" Salli said eagerly.

"If you're willing to get into the whole Hollywood sex machine deal. If you were *really* truthful,
we could probably have an intriguing piece. I'm
sure you've got lots of tales to tell."

"You should *hear* some of my stories," Salli said,

rolling her eyes. "I could lay stuff on you that'd make your tonsils hurt! Guys in this town—ha! There's *nothing* I don't know."

"Maybe I should talk to my editor."

"Wow!" Salli said, wriggling in her seat. "Can I be on the cover?"

"We have twelve covers a year," Madison explained. "Only four of those are show-business-related. That's a tough prize to win."

"Every magazine wants me on the cover," Salli said guilelessly. "Truth is, I sell magazines."

"I'm sure. But my editor walks his own path."

"Remember those pictures of Demi Moore on the front of *Vanity Fair*—all naked and pregnant?" Salli said brightly. "I heard it *zoomed* their circulation. How about *me* naked? Would your editor go for that?"

Madison shook her head. "More *Playboy* than us."

Salli giggled. "I *know*. Only joking. I've been on *Playboy*'s cover three times. They adore me." She giggled again. "Or rather, they adore my big boobs!"

"I can imagine you're very popular."

"Why are you coming to L.A.?" Salli asked.

"I'm interviewing Freddie Leon, the agent. You don't happen to know him, do you?"

"Wow! Freddie Leon," Salli sighed. "He's the man."

"I take it he's high on your list of important people?"

"Freddie Leon is only the most powerful agent in Hollywood," Salli said reverently, nodding as she said it, her blond curls bouncing. "My ambition is that one day he'll represent *me.*"

"Have you ever met him?" Madison asked curiously.

Salli hesitated before answering. "Well," she said tentatively, "once . . . a while ago."

"Yes?" Madison encouraged, sensing a story. "What happened?"

"I wasn't his type," Salli said flatly, as if the memory didn't please her.

Madison sensed a story. "Sexually? Or as a potential client?" she asked.

Salli wriggled in her seat. "One day I kinda tracked him in the underground parking of his office. He gave me the big brush." She frowned. "Maybe he's not into sex, 'cause believe me—I do *not* get turndowns—I mean like *never!*"

"You went there to have sex with him?" Madison asked, surprised at her openness.

"No!" Salli answered indignantly. "I went there to get his attention. I wasn't married then, my career was going nowhere, so I was taking a shot."

Madison decided that Salli's honesty was quite refreshing. There was a certain girlish naïveté hidden beneath the bleached blond hair and outrageous boobs.

"Are we nearly there?" Salli inquired, beginning to get nervous.

"Yes," Madison said. "Time to prepare yourself.

35

Remember what I told you—close your eyes, take a long, deep breath and slowly count to a hundred. I'll let you know when we're on the ground."

"You're the best!" Salli exclaimed. "Truth is, I don't have any girlfriends, they're all jealous." She gave a wan little smile. "Dunno why—they could have what I have for a price. Well, not *everything,*" she added thoughtfully. "They certainly couldn't have Bobby—he's totally yummy and all mine!"

"How long have you been married?"

"Exactly six months, two weeks, three days and, if I had a watch, I'd probably say thirty-three seconds." She laughed, slightly embarrassed. "I don't sound *too* much in love, do I?"

"What does Bobby do?"

"He's like a major danger adventure guy. Rides motorcycles and cars, stuff like that. Jumps over, like, forty-two buses. All the things someone called Evel Knievel did years and years ago, in my grandma's day."

"Oh, yes, I've read about him. Bobby Skorch. The man who takes his life in his hands every day."

"That's my Bobby," Salli said proudly. "Are *you* married?"

Madison shook her head. "Too scary for me," she said, thinking briefly of David, who'd never asked. For two years they'd been inseparable; now they were total strangers.

"I was married before Bobby," Salli announced. "To a psycho freakazoid *asshole* actor."

Madison laughed. "Tell me how you *really* feel."

Salli frowned again, thinking about her ex. "He

sued *me* for alimony. Can you believe it? He *still* thinks that one day I'll take him back. Moron *city!"*

"How long were you married to him?"

"Long enough for the bastard to break my arm a couple of times. Not to mention black eyes and bruises and all of that."

"Sounds like a charmer."

"He thought he was."

Salli didn't speak again until the plane landed. Then she opened her eyes and unbuckled her seat belt. "That was a cinch!" she exclaimed. "Want a job as my flying coach?"

Madison smiled. "Think I'll pass," she said, standing up and stretching.

"If you don't have anybody meeting you, we can give you a ride in our limo," Salli offered. "Bobby's into the extra extra stretch with the Jacuzzi in the back. It's *sooo* Hollywood, but since we're both from little towns, we get off on it!"

"That's okay," Madison said, still smiling. "My friend's picking me up."

"You've *got* to come visit me," Salli said, scribbling her number on a menu and handing it over. "You're *sooo* cool—and great-looking too, in a kind of like *normal* way."

Madison laughed. *"Thanks,* I think!"

"I mean it," Salli said enthusiastically. "Our house in the Palisades is *amazing."*

"I'm sure."

"Oh, God!" Salli groaned, with an exaggerated shudder. "Here comes the letch."

And Bo Deacon was upon them, all washed and

brushed—and drenched in a heavy cologne. He attempted to take Salli's arm, but she was too quick for him, niftily backing into a burly businessman who couldn't be more delighted that he actually got to touch the delectable Salli T. Turner.

An airline rep pushed past, eager to reach his two stars. Madison heard Bo say to Salli in a nasty whisper, "What's the matter, bitch? Trying to forget the people who got you where you are today?"

Madison shook her head and exited the plane, walking briskly through the airport to the luggage carousel.

"Girlfriend!" Natalie yelled, appearing out of nowhere. "You're here!"

Madison was delighted to see her. *"Finally,"* she said with a big grin. "It was a long flight."

They exchanged warm hugs.

"The traffic was a monster," Natalie said. "I only just made it."

"You saved me a limo ride."

"How's that?"

Madison indicated Salli T. Turner and Bobby Skorch locked in a steamy embrace by the exit. "I could've hitched a ride with them."

"No way," Natalie said disbelievingly. "The delectable Salli T. Queen of the wet dream brigade."

"I certainly could've. Salli's my new best friend."

Natalie laughed. "Does that mean you've traded my fine black ass for a bountiful blonde?"

"Yeah, right," Madison said dryly. "Can't you

imagine me and Salli T. palling out? We've got so much in common."

"Hmm . . ." Natalie said, staring over. "The husband's pretty damn cute."

Madison glanced at Salli and Bobby, who were still making out, in spite of—or maybe because of—several hovering paparazzi. "All I can see is black leather, long hair, and tattoos."

Natalie gave a dirty laugh. "Sometimes I like 'em rough and colorful."

Oh, God, Madison thought. *Shades of college. We've only been together two minutes and we're already discussing men.*

"Here comes my suitcase," she said, lugging it off the moving carousel. "Let's go."

"Before you succumb to the limo ride?" Natalie teased.

"Don't be ridiculous!" Madison replied, laughing.

Within minutes they were in Natalie's car, heading for the Hollywood Hills, where Natalie shared a small house with her brother, Cole, a personal trainer.

Madison gazed out the window. Sunshine, palm trees, fast food restaurants and gas stations. Ah, L.A., what a place!

In spite of her misgivings about Hollywood and its inhabitants, she was excited about her assignment. Freddie Leon was a high-profile power broker who'd managed to keep an exceptionally low profile in his private life. One wife. Two children. No scandal. And yet here was a man who controlled the most important talent in Hollywood. A man who had everyone's attention.

She was determined to find out everything— unearth the real man beneath the impenetrable image.

It was a challenge.

Madison always *had* relished a challenge.

chapter 6

"I'M LEAVING NOW," FREDDIE Leon informed his executive assistant, Ria Santiago.

Ria glanced up from her desk as Freddie passed by. She was an attractive Hispanic woman in her mid-forties who'd worked for Freddie for just over ten years. She knew him as well as anyone—which didn't mean a lot, because Freddie was an intensely private person who was all business.

"Shall I phone Mrs. Leon and tell her you're on your way?" Ria inquired, tapping a sharp pencil on her desktop.

"No," Freddie said. "I have to make a stop. I'll call her myself from the car."

"Very well," Ria replied, knowing better than to ask where he was going.

Freddie stepped into the private elevator he shared with his partner in I.A.A., Max Steele, and pressed the button for underground parking. When he stepped off the elevator, his maroon Rolls was waiting, waxed and gleaming, which pleased him because he was very particular about his cars—the slightest scrape or blemish drove him insane.

Willie, the parking valet, jumped to attention. "Weatherman says it might rain, Mr. Leon," Willie said cheerfully, careful to breathe in the other direction lest the Scotch he'd just swigged from the bottle hit Freddie in the face.

"The weatherman is wrong, Willie. I can smell rain when it's on the way."

"Yessir, Mr. Leon," Willie said respectfully, backing away even further. He knew how to kiss ass better than anyone; it got him a five-hundred-buck cash tip every Christmas.

Freddie got in his car and drove carefully from the I.A.A. building—an architectural delight—his mind running over the events of the day, making sure he remembered every detail. The less committed to paper the better—that was Freddie's philosophy. It had worked well for him over the years.

He hoped Lucinda Bennett was not about to cause trouble. He'd negotiated a major contract for her—more money than she'd ever received before—and with Kevin Page as her costar, their movie together was bound to be a hit. Now Lucinda was attempting to give him a hard time, which wouldn't work—his little remark about the negatives in his safe had definitely given her something to think about.

What kind of Hollywood was it today when he had to talk an actress, whose career would be over in less than five years, into accepting twelve million dollars?

Talent. They were a breed unto themselves. Egotistical, ungrateful and predictable. Which is why Freddie was able to convince them he was always right. Deep down they were children who needed tough love and guidance. Freddie gave them exactly what they wanted. Max was his complete opposite. Max was Mr. Smoothie. Divorced and always on the lookout for fresh new talent, Max cultivated the playboy image—a racy Porsche, a wardrobe of Brioni suits, a penthouse apartment on Wilshire, and countless beautiful women. The difference between them worked. Freddie handled the major superstars, Max looked after the slightly lower-level luminaries.

Freddie smiled to himself, a smile that did not reach his lips. Max thought he was the smartest guy in town; in truth he was a joke—Freddie's own private source of amusement—for nobody fooled Freddie Leon. And Freddie knew for a fact that for the last three months Max had been involved in secret negotiations to land a high-powered studio job. And if he snagged it he'd leave I.A.A. and Freddie without a backward glance, selling his interest in I.A.A. to the highest bidder.

Freddie had his own future to watch out for. Max

Steele was a traitor. And Freddie knew how to deal with traitors better than anyone.

Oblivious to Freddie Leon's knowledge of his negotiations, Max Steele wound up a long lunch at the Grill. His luncheon companion was a breathtakingly beautiful Swedish model who bore more than a passing resemblance to a young Grace Kelly.

Inga Cruelle wanted to make the difficult transition from supermodel to movie star.

Max Steele wanted to get into her Victoria's Secret lacy thong and fuck the life out of her.

They both had their agendas.

"So you see," Inga said, as they lingered over decaf cappuccinos, her long delicate fingers toying with the rim of her coffee cup, "I do not wish to do what Cindy did. A starring role will be too difficult for my first attempt."

The ego on these girls was astounding, Max thought. However beautiful she was, what made Inga Cruelle imagine she could cut it on the big screen when there were hundreds of actresses out there—girls who really knew their craft—who couldn't even get in for an audition?

"Very wise," he said. Max was not movie-star handsome, but at forty-two he had an abundance of boyish charm, a full head of curly brown hair, an in-shape body and plenty of style. Plus his reputation as a cocksman was legendary.

"Elle seems to be doing it the right way," Inga mused, her long tapered fingers now twirling her coffee spoon. "She was quite good in the Streisand movie."

This was their second lunch together, and Max had played his role perfectly. They were the agent and the potential client. Nothing more. By this time Inga—who was used to reducing most men to slobbering idiots—must be wondering why he hadn't made any kind of move.

"Elle's a smart girl," he said briskly. "She works hard."

"*I'll* work hard," Inga said, her exquisite unmade-up face painfully earnest. "I'll even take acting classes if you think it's necessary."

No, sweetheart. Why would you want to do that? You're a successful model. Don't put yourself out.

"Right," he said. "Good idea."

"You are so understanding, Max, so helpful," Inga said, placing a delicate hand on his arm.

Good. She was making the first move.

"Listen," he said as sincerely as he could manage. "I want to help you, Inga, so I'm sending you to see a director friend of mine. Maybe, if he likes you, I can persuade him to shoot a test."

"A screen test?"

"Yeah, get a feeling of how you are in front of the camera."

Inga laughed, as if it was the most ridiculous thing she'd ever heard. "You've seen my photographs, Max," she said immodestly. "You *know* the camera loves and adores me."

"Still photographs are different. The movie camera has a mind of its own," Max said, marveling at her conceit. *"You* brought up Cindy. Yeah, sure she's a knockout, and she *looked* fantastic in her movie. But the big problem was her emotions simply didn't translate. She came across as a blank canvas."

"That is *exactly* why I do not wish to *star* in my first film," Inga said, as if producers were lining up to hire her.

"I could also set something up on a social level," Max said casually, baiting the trap. "Maybe a dinner at the Leons'."

"Your partner?"

"Freddie's dinners are legendary."

"Very well," Inga said. "Should I bring my fiancé?"

What was with this fiancé crap? It was the first *he'd* heard of it.

"I didn't know you were engaged," he said, slightly irritated.

"My fiancé lives in Sweden," Inga said, her precise accent a definite detriment to a film career. "He is arriving tomorrow to spend two days with me at the Bel Air Hotel, then he will fly home."

"Really?" Max said, even more irritated. "What does he do?"

"He's a very successful businessman," Inga replied. "We have known each other since school."

Max was not interested in the details. "When are you returning to New York?" he asked, wondering if she gave great head.

"Perhaps next week," Inga said. "My agency is impatient. However, I told them how important it is that I stay here until I have made a decision about my movie commitments."

"Sounds good to me," Max said, deciding that she probably didn't. Beautiful girls were not as into it as their plainer sisters. "Only I should warn you," he added, "no fiancés at business meetings. Leave him at the hotel."

"This will not be a problem," Inga said coolly.

Max snapped his fingers for the check, which the waiter immediately brought to the table.

So, she has a fiancé, he thought. *Am I wasting my time or what?*

No, she also has that hungry look. The look all these girls have when they want to be movie stars.

"Time to get back to work," he said, signing the check and standing up.

Inga slid out of the booth. She had on white slacks and a pale pink angora sweater, which gently covered the swell of her small, perfect breasts. He knew they were perfect and not silicone-enhanced, because he'd seen the nude spread she'd done for famed photographer Helmut Newton in *Vogue.* Eight pages of Inga. Black stockings, matching garter belt, stiletto heels, and a Great Dane sitting passively at her feet. Very classy. Very naked. Not at all crude.

Max decided the time had come to nail this delectable Swedish morsel. He wanted to go down on her—his specialty—in the worst way.

And soon.

Fiancé or no fiancé, he had no doubt she was a sure thing.

chapter 7

KRISTIN DID NOT POS-
sess white hose, which meant a trip to Neiman
Marcus. Not such a hardship, as she enjoyed strolling around the luxurious store buying clothes she
didn't need and perusing the tempting makeup
counters. Shopping was therapeutic—it took her
mind off everything, suspending her in a land of
soft, sensual lingerie, Judith Leiber purses and
Manolo Blahnik shoes.

Recently they'd installed a huge curved martini
bar in the men's department. Kristin felt comfortable sitting at it, sipping a vodka martini, daydreaming that she was a perfect Hollywood wife
with two darling little children and an important
executive big-deal husband. A *faithful* big-deal hus-

band—because all the ones she came across were lying whoremongers who cheated on their wives without giving their infidelities a second thought. And Kristin should know—she'd had most of them in the three years she'd been a call girl in Hollywood.

Kristin and her younger sister, Cherie, had arrived in L.A. four years ago, with aspirations to become movie stars. Kristin had been nineteen, Cherie eighteen, and like hundreds and thousands of teenage hopefuls before them, they'd saved their money, left the small town they'd lived in all their young lives, and made the trek west in a beat-up Volkswagen.

Cherie was the true beauty of the family—or so everyone always said. Kristin was merely the sister who paled in comparison. But the two of them were the closest of friends, and did everything together.

As soon as they arrived in L.A. they rented a cheap apartment and both got jobs waitressing in a busy Italian restaurant on Melrose. Cherie lasted exactly one week before being discovered by one of the customers—Howie Powers—the bad-boy son of a rich business executive.

From the start Kristin knew that Howie was not good news. She found out he was heavily into drugs, booze and gambling. She also discovered he was into taking his father's money and blowing it on fast cars and as many women as he could handle. That is, until he spotted Cherie, and fell in love.

Howie pursued Cherie relentlessly, taking her to the best restaurants and clubs, showering her with expensive presents, treating her like a queen. It wasn't long before he persuaded her to give up her job and move in with him. Kristin warned her not to, but Cherie wouldn't listen. "He wants to marry me," she said, all starry-eyed and in love. "We're doing it after I meet his parents."

"And when will that be?" Kristin asked.

"Soon," Cherie replied. "He's taking me to Palm Springs to see them."

Kristin didn't believe it for a moment. Howie wasn't the marrying kind. He'd string Cherie along with promises until he grew tired of her, and then he'd dump her. Kristin knew the type—she'd experienced the rich-boy syndrome in high school when she'd given up her virginity to the captain of the football team and he'd boasted to everyone about his conquest. When she'd complained, he'd refused to speak to her again. A sobering lesson about men.

Kristin saw Howie as the sleazy playboy he was—especially when one day he came on to *her* while Cherie was out shopping. She loathed him, but at the same time she was forced to put up with him because of her sister. Until the night she discovered that Howie had gotten Cherie hooked on cocaine. Then she went crazy, fighting with both of them. Cherie told her to back off and mind her own business. So she did.

And two weeks later she'd gotten a midnight call informing her that on their way to Palm Springs to meet his parents, Howie had fallen asleep at the wheel of his Porsche, crossed the dividing line of the highway and smashed head-on into another car. The driver of the other car was killed, Howie was only slightly injured, and Cherie was in a coma.

Now it was four years later, and Cherie lay in a nursing home—a virtual vegetable—while Kristin was one of the most successful call girls in town. She'd had no choice; somebody had to pay the hospital bills, and that somebody certainly wasn't Howie Powers—who'd instantly vanished out of their lives.

"Excuse me, do you mind if I sit here?"

Kristin glanced up. A man had settled on the stool next to her, in spite of the fact that there were many empty places. He was handsome in a rumpled way—not at all Beverly Hills or Bel Air. He had on a white T-shirt, brown leather flying jacket, khaki pants and well-worn sneakers.

"Not at all," she replied carefully, wondering if he'd ever been a customer. Highly unlikely; he didn't look like a man who had to pay for it.

"I'm not coming out with a line," he said in a deep husky voice. "But can I ask you a big favor?"

No favors, honey. Cash up front. I have bills to pay.

"What?" she said shortly.

"This'll *sound* like a line," he said, grinning. "Only believe me—it's not. You see, I gotta go to my father's wedding, and I haven't worn a tie in years, not to mention the fact that when it comes to clothes I have no taste. So . . ." He thrust two ties in front of her. "Whaddya think?"

"What do *I* think?" she said slowly.

"Yes. I need an opinion other than my own. And you look like a woman with an eye for the best."

"Why don't you ask a salesperson?" she suggested.

"'Cause they don't have your class and style," he said, his grin widening. *"You* will make me into the son my dad always wanted."

It was so long since she'd experienced a genuine pickup that she couldn't help smiling. "You're not from L.A., are you?" she said.

"Nope," he replied. "Arizona. Drove here yesterday. The wedding's on Sunday. What's your pick?"

She stared at the two ties, both boringly conservative. "Come with me," she said, standing up. "I'm sure we can do better." And with that she led him toward the tie department.

An hour later, with a purple Armani tie in his shopping bag, they were still talking. She'd found out his name was Jake and he was a professional photographer—much to his banker father's disgust. He was thirty, unmarried and had moved to L.A. to pursue a new job with a magazine.

"The money's great," he said. "And it'll be a challenge photographing real humans instead of animals and landscapes."

"Real humans? *Here?"* Kristin drawled, sipping her third martini. "You *do* know you're in L.A."

"Don't sound so jaded," he said, "it doesn't go with your looks."

What the hell are you doing? she asked herself crossly. *Sitting here flirting with a total stranger. And actually liking it.*

"I have to go," she said abruptly, standing up.

"Why?" he asked, standing too. "Is there a husband I should know about?"

No, honey. There's a career you wouldn't want to know about. I'm for sale. Lock, stock and fine ass.

"A . . . fiancé," she lied, pushing the door firmly shut. "And he's *very* jealous."

"Don't blame him," Jake said, giving her a long lingering look.

She felt a jolt of unexpected excitement and wondered what it would be like to sleep with a man who wasn't a paying client.

Don't even think about it. You're a whore—making money. And that's all *you're interested in.*

"Uh . . . good luck with the wedding," she said.

"It's his fourth," Jake said. "He's sixty-two. The bride's twenty."

"I'm sure your tie'll look great."

"Why wouldn't it? You chose it."

They exchanged another long look, before she forced herself to move off toward the escalator.

Just as she was stepping on, he came after her. "I'm staying at the Sunset Marquis," he said. "I wish you'd call me. I'd really love to take your picture sometime."

She nodded. *No chance of that.*

"Goodbye, Jake," she said.

It wouldn't do to be late for Mister X.

chapter 8

MADISON WAS ON THE phone. "So?" she said, holding the receiver away from her ear because her editor, Victor, always spoke in an overly loud, booming voice, one capable of shattering eardrums. "When am I getting my interview with Freddie Leon?"

"You just arrived, didn't you?"

"Stepped off the plane an hour ago."

"What's *wrong* with you?" Victor said loudly. "Can't you settle down for a couple of days and relax like everyone else?"

"I'm not in a relaxing frame of mind, Victor. I'm here to work."

"All work and no play . . ."

"Don't give me that cliché bullshit," she said

crisply. "Besides, you should be thrilled I'm a total workaholic." A short pause to let him think about *that* for a moment. "Now," she continued crisply. "When do I get to meet him?"

Victor sighed. "You're an impossible woman."

"Never said I wasn't."

"My contact's out of town until tomorrow."

"Wonderful timing."

"Nobody's perfect. Only you."

"Glad you realize it."

"Okay, okay, tomorrow I'll get it set. That's a promise."

"Good." She hesitated a moment before continuing. "Uh . . . by the way, Victor, this is a kind of off-the-wall suggestion . . ."

"Let me hear it."

"Well, on the plane I was sitting next to Salli T. Turner."

"Lucky you!" Victor boomed.

"I wasn't sure you'd know who I was talking about."

"My eleven-year-old son and I watch *Teach!* every Tuesday night. Kind of a male-bonding thing."

"How sweet."

"There's nothing *sweet* about Salli T. Turner," Victor chuckled, sounding uncharacteristically lecherous. "As my son would say—'she's the shit!'"

"Victor!"

"Sorry," he boomed. "Did I just get carried away?"

"You certainly did," Madison said, laughing. "Totally unlike you."

"What is it you wanted to tell me about her?"

"Actually, I was thinking she might make a good interview."

"You'd be prepared to interview Salli T. Turner?" Victor asked, barely able to conceal his surprise.

"Why not? She's refreshingly honest, and I'm sure she'd be prepared to reveal *plenty* about what goes on in Hollywood if you're a young, gorgeous babe with . . . uh . . . quite remarkable assets. It would definitely be a feminist piece with a twist. What do you think?"

"I think if *you* like the idea, we should give it a shot."

"Good. I can fit it in while I'm sitting around waiting for Mr. Leon."

"For chrissakes, Madison, stop complaining. I'll get back to you A.S.A.P."

"Do that," she said, replacing the receiver with a grin.

"What's up?" Natalie asked, handing her a glass of cold apple juice.

"Victor's got a yen for Salli T. Can you imagine? Victor *never* looks at any woman other than Evelyn."

"And Evelyn is . . . ?"

"His wife, of course. Rules him with an iron fist and a handy riding crop."

Natalie giggled. "You mean he likes to get his powerful little butt whacked?"

"Not so little," Madison answered, smiling back. "Victor's like a big cuddly bear. *Definitely* not an L.A. bod."

Natalie glanced at her watch. "Damn!" she said, grabbing her jacket. "I gotta get to the studio. Anything you need?"

"Don't worry about me," Madison said calmly. "I'm the perfect houseguest. Put me next to a phone and I'm content."

"Cole'll be home soon."

"I haven't seen him in years."

"Then you're in for a shock," Natalie said crisply. "You probably remember him as a skinny, strung-out hyper teen monster. Right?"

"Right," Madison agreed, remembering how Natalie always used to despair because her younger brother was heavily into rap, gangs and getting high.

"Now he's Mr. Focused. In fact, he's one of the most in-demand fitness trainers in L.A. Oh yeah," Natalie added, as she reached the door. "*And* he came out of the closet. See you later."

Cole was in the closet? Funky little Cole with his punk attitude and macho swagger. Madison shook her head . . . who would've guessed? Certainly not she.

Reaching for the phone, she tried the number Salli had given her. No reply, so with nothing else to do, she went in the tiny guest room and unpacked her one suitcase. She could have stayed at a hotel—Victor was quite generous with expenses—but Natalie would have been disappointed. Besides, she *wanted* to stay with her best friend, it was probably the only time they'd get to spend together all year. And they certainly had plenty to catch up on. Madison couldn't wait to get down with some good old girl talk.

At six she clicked on the TV to catch Natalie's entertainment spot on the news. The male news anchor was impossibly handsome, with a dazzling smile. His co-anchor was a young blond Joan Lunden clone. The weatherman was Hispanic. And then on came Natalie with her show-business news, sparkling with her own particular brand of personality and charm.

"I *hate* doing all that gossip crap," Natalie had confided in the car on the way in from the airport. "But at least it gets my face on TV and it's good experience."

Just as Natalie was finishing her spot, Cole walked in. Or at least Madison assumed it was Cole, although this tall, muscled Denzel Washington look-alike in workout shorts and a Lakers tank bore no resemblance to the lanky teen rebel she'd last seen when she and Natalie graduated college seven years ago.

"Cole?" she questioned.

"Madison?" he answered.

And they grinned at each other, exchanging "You look greats!" and "It's been so long!"

What a waste, Madison thought, checking him out. Why were all the truly gorgeous ones gay?

"Got everything you need?" Cole asked, swigging from a plastic bottle of Evian.

"I told your sister—give me a phone and I'm happy."

"You here on business?"

"I write for *Manhattan Style*. Profiles on Power."

"Who're you nailing?"

"Freddie Leon, the agent."

"Cool guy."

"You know him?"

"Gave the dude a private session once when his regular guy was sick. Man, he was into it big time."

"A jock, huh?"

"Competitive, that's the vibe I got." Another swig of Evian. "Y'know, I train his partner, Max Steele."

"You do!" Madison exclaimed, sensing a major break. "Cole! I think I love you!"

"Huh?"

"Max Steele's number one on the list of people I need to talk to. When can you set it up?"

"Hey," Cole said, laughing. "Hold on—I said I train him, I do *not* arrange his schedule."

"All I need is a fast half hour," Madison said, eyes gleaming.

"Max is a busy dude, always runnin' somewhere."

"Of course, I *could* set it up through the magazine," Madison mused. "But if *you* arrange it for me, it'll be so much quicker."

"We run the UCLA track every morning at seven A.M. Whyn't you jog on by an' I'll intro you."

"That's a great idea! I'll be there."

"Yeah . . . an' wear somethin' hot, he's into the femmes."

Now it was Madison's turn to laugh. "I want to *talk* to him, not fuck him!"

Cole grinned. "Hey—you never know . . . he's a real player."

Madison mock frowned. "Behave yourself. I knew you when you were nothing more than a horny delinquent!"

Cole's grin widened. "Yeah, well, nothing much has changed. 'Cept now I'm horny in the opposite direction."

"So Natalie told me."

He grabbed an apple from the counter. "She kinda gets a buzz from it—y'know, her brother, the fruit. When the two of us go out we take bets on which guys are straight an' which ones dance with Dorothy. I fake her out every time, 'cause my instincts *rule!*"

After Cole went off to shower, Madison tried Salli again. This time Salli answered her phone, all breathy-voiced. "Hi," she said. "This is Salli T."

"Remember me?" Madison said. "Your flying coach."

"*'Course* I do," Salli said, sounding pleased. "Wow! You're actually calling me. Didn't think you would."

"I spoke to my editor. He loves the idea of an interview."

"That was quick."

"Very. Can I come by sometime after twelve tomorrow?"

"Well . . ." Salli said hesitantly. "I really *should* tell my publicist. He'll be mad at me if I arrange something on my own."

"Publicists have a habit of screwing everything

up," Madison said crisply, trying to discourage her because dealing with publicists was a total pain in the ass. "Do it if you want, but I should warn you, by the time he gets into it, I'll probably be long gone."

"You're right," Salli agreed. "And I *do* want to be in *Manhattan Style*. It will be like a kind of new image thing for me, right?"

"We'll have fun," Madison promised.

"Okay," Salli said, like a little kid planning something naughty. "I'll give you my address and you can come to lunch tomorrow."

"Looking forward to it."

And she was. There was something very appealing about Salli T. Turner. In spite of the obvious sex-bomb presentation—big boobs and clouds of bleached hair—she had a certain sweetness and vulnerability. A kind of early Marilyn Monroe quality.

Madison used her laptop to E-mail New York, requesting a clippings file on Salli. Then she checked out her copious notes on Freddie Leon, and finally relaxed, adding a slug of vodka to her boringly healthy apple juice as she kicked back in front of the TV and waited for Natalie to get home.

L.A. was turning out to be better than she'd thought.

chapter 9

ON IMPULSE FREDDIE Leon decided to stop by Lucinda Bennett's Bel Air mansion. He was tired of waiting for the signed contracts, tired of being prisoner to her capricious will. He didn't usually make house calls, but since Lucinda was being so difficult, he felt a little hand-holding might be in order. *Hold a child's hand and you can lead them wherever you want*—his father had told him that when he was thirteen, and he'd never forgotten. Yes, it was time to put an end to all this nonsense, as only he could.

Nellie, Lucinda's faithful Bahamian housekeeper, answered the door. "Why, Mr. Leon, what *you* doin' here?" Nellie asked, throwing up her massive arms as if to ward him off. "Madam—she no expectin' you."

"Correct, she's not," Freddie agreed, handing her the three dozen red roses he had prudently purchased at Flower Fashions on the way. "Put these in a vase, Nellie, and give them to her. Tell her I'll be waiting in the living room."

"She be in the middle of a foot massage," Nellie confided.

"I'm sure you can disturb her," Freddie replied, striding into the tastefully decorated living room, overlooking a cool blue infinity pool. Lucinda owned several houses; this one in Bel Air was his favorite. He stood by the window staring out, aware that he might have a long wait. Knowing Lucinda, she'd have to get herself together, check her makeup, hair, clothes. Lucinda was one of the old-fashioned breed of stars, unlike the young actresses today who slumped into his office looking like they'd just stepped out of somebody's bed. Angela Musconni was the hottest young star around, and when Max Steele had encountered her leaving Freddie's office last week, he'd grabbed his partner by the arm and whispered in his ear, "You *gotta* be kidding? I wouldn't fuck her with somebody else's dick." Trust Max to say exactly what everyone else was thinking. Angela looked like a heroin addict on the run, but she was an excellent actress.

After twenty-five minutes Lucinda made her entrance. She was a tall woman with dramatic features and smooth, pale red hair worn in a becoming bob. She was not traditionally beautiful, more striking with her aquiline nose and piercing eyes, but her talent was ferocious and her fans equally so. Lucinda had been a star for almost twenty years.

"And to what do I owe this honor?" Lucinda asked, sweeping into the room, resplendent in a pale beige cashmere pantsuit and extremely high heels.

"I'm playing errand boy today," Freddie said, kissing her on both cheeks.

Her finely penciled eyebrows shot up. "Freddie Leon—errand boy? I can hardly believe it."

"Believe it, sweetheart. I'm well aware of how insecure you get, so I'm here to personally pick up your signed contract."

Lucinda's finely rouged scarlet lips pursed dramatically. "Really?"

"Lucinda, dear, you should know better than anyone, there is *no way* I would push you into anything that wasn't right for you."

Lucinda collapsed into an overstuffed chair, kicking off her shoes like a petulant ten-year-old. "It's not that I'm being difficult, Freddie," she said. "It's simply that I don't want to look . . . foolish."

"How could *you* possibly look foolish?" Freddie asked forcefully.

"Well, Dmitri said—"

"Who's Dmitri?" he interrupted.

"Someone I've been seeing," she said, becoming uncharacteristically coy.

Oh God, now he got it. She had a new man in her life, and like the legions before him, he was putting in his ten cents. "Have I met Dmitri?" he asked.

"No," Lucinda replied, still verging on the coy side. "But you will."

"I'm sure," Freddie said. "Is he around today?"

"He's out by the pool," Lucinda said. "Let's not disturb him, he might be sleeping."

God, no! Freddie thought. *Let's not disturb him if he's working on a tan. Jesus! Where do these women find these men?*

"Have I told you that you look incredibly beautiful today?" Freddie said, lightening his strategy.

"No," Lucinda said, slightly flustered. "As a matter of fact you haven't."

"Well, you do. You're my most important client and that's why I'm here." He began pacing. "Sign the contract, Lucinda. Otherwise, this deal is about to fall through, and I wouldn't want that happening to you."

She hesitated. He could sense that she was almost his—not quite. "But Dmitri said that if I was to star opposite Kevin Page, it might make me appear . . . older."

"You—older?" Freddie shook his head. "Every young guy in America will be *wishing* he was in Kevin Page's shoes."

"Yes?"

"Come along, Lucinda, let's go in your office, sign the contract and then I can get on with my day."

"If you're *really* sure . . ."

"Have I ever guided you wrong?"

Fifteen minutes later he was back in his car with the signed contracts on the seat beside him. Sometimes a little personal attention was all that was needed. And for a twelve-million-dollar deal, Freddie didn't mind putting out.

The two men playing racquetball were going at it with a "take no prisoners" attitude. Both men were in their forties, and very fit; even so the vigorous workout was making them sweat profusely.

Max Steele slammed the final shot, clinching the game. "Fifty bucks!" he yelled triumphantly. "And I want cash."

Howie Powers slumped against the wall. He was a sandy-haired man in his thirties, with crooked features, a stocky build and a permanent tan. "Shit, Max!" he complained, irritated at being beaten. "You gotta win at everything?"

"And what's wrong with that?" Max said cheerfully. "No point in playing if you don't plan on winning."

Howie stood up straight. "I might go to Vegas for the day tomorrow. Wanna come?" he offered. "We can hop a ride on my dad's plane, he's goin' on business."

"Don't you ever work?" Max said, grabbing a towel as they made their way to the locker room.

"Work? What's that?" Howie said, smirking.

Max shook his head. "Beats me why I hang with a bum like you," he grumbled. "You're useless."

"Why would I *wanna* work?" Howie questioned, genuinely puzzled. "I got plenty of bucks."

"Yeah, handouts from your old man."

"You're forgetting my trust fund," Howie said, with another satisfied smirk. "Who needs handouts? I only take 'em 'cause my old man insists."

"Aren't you ever bored?" Max asked, thinking how much he would hate having nothing substantial to do.

"Bored?" Howie said with a manic laugh. "You gotta be shittin' me. There's not enough time in the day to cover all the things I do."

Max nodded knowingly. "Yeah, like uh . . . go to the track, hang with the guys, play poker, smoke some primo grass, pick up girls, gamble, do a little coke, go out and get drunk . . ."

"Sounds like a life to me," Howie said, the smirk creeping back onto his face.

"I'm into work," Max said forcefully. "I get off on the power."

"You—you're an overachiever," Howie said. "Me—I'm into getting my rocks off while I can still get it up!"

Max thought to himself that if *he'd* been born with a silver spoon up his ass, he'd probably enjoy the good life, too. But he'd had to work for everything he'd achieved—starting off in the mail room at William Morris, where he'd hooked up with Freddie. A fortunate meeting, for the two of them had risen together, until they'd made their break ten years ago and started their own agency. Now they were one of the top three agencies in town. In fact, right at this moment I.A.A. represented the biggest stars, the hottest screenwriters *and* the best directors and producers in Hollywood.

And yet in spite of their well-earned success, for quite a while now Max had been thinking of making a change. Being an agent was one thing, but running a studio would give him a lot more of the power he craved. Hey, if guys like Jon Peters could do it, he was in like a sailor in a room full of hookers.

The only problem was telling Freddie, who had no idea he was thinking of defecting, and would throw a total shit-fit when he told him of his plans. But that was nothing Max couldn't handle.

Not a word until the deal was done. Only then would he think of the perfect way out.

chapter 10

NATALIE RUSHED IN FROM the studio all smiles. "Did you catch me on TV?" she asked enthusiastically. "How about the bit I did on Salli T. and Bo Deacon?"

"Must have missed that," Madison said. "What did you say?"

"Oh, I said something like, 'Guess who flew into L.A. together,' you know—provocative inside gossip. The audience loves it."

"They *weren't* together," Madison pointed out.

"Who cares?" Natalie said airily. "They're both publicity hounds. They'll get off hearing their names mentioned."

"If you say so," Madison murmured, not so sure that Salli would be thrilled.

"I *know* so," Natalie said confidently. "You should read some of the letters I get—all they want is the dirt."

"That's sad."

"No. That's just how it is."

"If you say so," Madison murmured.

"C'mon," Natalie said, full of energy. "Move your butt, I'm buying you dinner and hearing all about what happened with you and David."

"It's a short story," Madison said crisply.

"Good. You tell me yours, I'll tell you mine. Oh, did you get to see Cole?"

"I certainly did," Madison said, grabbing her purse. "He came home, jumped in the shower, took off again and told me to tell you he won't be home tonight."

Natalie rolled her eyes disapprovingly. "He met some big showbiz executive—the type who picks a boy of the month. Trouble is Cole won't hear anything against him."

"You're not his mother—don't try to run his life—*especially* his love life."

"Ain't *that* the truth," Natalie sighed, as they headed for the door. "But hey—I'm *way* more street smart than he is, he *should* listen."

"He told me he trains Freddie Leon's partner, Max Steele," Madison said.

"Didn't I mention it?"

"No, you didn't. But Cole said if I'm on the jogging track at UCLA at seven in the morning, he'll introduce me."

"Seven!" Natalie wailed, opening up her car door. "Honey, don't count on *me* to fix you coffee."

They went to Dan Tana's for dinner and sat in a cozy booth.

"Did I tell you I'm doing a piece for the magazine on Salli T.?" Madison said, ordering a vodka martini because she felt like it, and knew it would guarantee a good night's sleep.

"Yes. Didn't old Victor get all excited when you mentioned her name?" Natalie said, requesting a beer.

Madison nodded. "I plan on getting her to talk about the men who run Hollywood—they all seem to have this thing about hookers and strippers with hearts of gold—y'know, Julia what's-her-name in *Pretty Woman*—the one with the big hair. And Demi Moore in *Striptease*. I want to get Salli's take on it."

"Good, you can give me all the leftovers," Natalie said, studying a menu. "I'll use them on my show."

"You're really into your show, huh?"

"Hmm," Natalie said, making a face. "Sometimes I am, sometimes I'm not. It's so predictable. All these people out there plugging books, movies and their goddamn exercise tapes—and *I* have to pretend as if I'm interested."

"What do you *want* to do?"

"Be a network news anchor, of course."

"Sounds like a plan."

"Yeah?" Natalie said ruefully. "How many black news anchors do *you* see?"

"Here's *my* philosophy," Madison said. "If you want something bad enough, you gotta go for it."

"Let's order," Natalie said. *"My* philosophy is— food solves a shitload of problems!"

A few sips of her martini and Madison began talking. "I think I genuinely loved David," she said wistfully. "But the truth is he got scared."

"Typical!" Natalie interrupted.

"Some men say they're okay with strong women, only when they find themselves with one, they can't handle the pressure," Madison continued. Natalie nodded her agreement. "We never talked about marriage," Madison added. "We were happy just being together. Until one day he went out for cigarettes and failed to come back." She paused, remembering, shaking her head because the memories were still painful. "The thing that hurt the most was that after he left, he ran off and married his high-school sweetheart. *That* was a *real* pisser."

"Girl, I know exactly what you mean," Natalie said. "Denzl and I had this great thing going until I woke up one morning and the slippery son of a bitch wasn't there. Nor was my CD collection, which, as you can imagine, *totally* freaked me. Losing him was one thing, but losing Marvin Gaye?"

They stared at each other and suddenly burst out laughing. "Who'd believe *this?"* Natalie exclaimed. "Two smart, hot-looking women like us, and we just got ourselves dumped!"

"At least we can laugh about it now."

"Maybe you can."

"You weren't supposed to be with Denzl," Madison said firmly. "And *I* wasn't supposed to be with David. Somebody bigger and better will come along."

"Hmm . . . bigger," Natalie said with a dirty laugh. "I like it!" Then she added a quick *"Not* that I'm interested in getting involved again."

"Me neither," Madison agreed. "All this double-standard crap about how only guys can go out and have sex whenever they want, and it doesn't mean a thing. Women can too. Why should *we* have to be in a relationship?"

"Right on!" Natalie agreed. "Give me a great-looking guy with a great body. We'll have great sex, and don't call me, I'll call you."

"Yes!" Madison said. "As long as you use a condom. Things sure have changed since we were in college."

"Oh, by the way," Natalie said. "The anchorman on my show asked us over to his house for dinner tomorrow night. I said we'd go. Okay with you?"

"You're not fixing me up I hope," Madison said suspiciously.

"He's married."

"In that case, okay. I am *not* into fix-ups."

A waiter hovered by their table. "The gentleman at the bar would like to buy you two ladies a bottle of champagne."

They both looked over. An aging playboy with an ill-fitting black toupee perched on top of his head waved merrily. "Tell the gentleman thanks, but no thanks," Madison said.

"Yeah, suggest he save his money for his old age," Natalie added. The waiter moved away. "That's the oldest pickup line in the world," Natalie said, grimacing. "Surely the poor old dude could come up with something more original?"

"Pickup lines are universal," Madison said wisely. "They go on forever."

"How much you wanna bet he'll come over spouting another corny line?"

Madison shook her head. "No balls," she said.

"Is that a rug he's wearing, or am I seeing things?" Natalie said, stifling a crazed giggle.

"Do *not* make eye contact," Madison warned, suppressing her own laughter. "Otherwise, he *will* come over, and then we'll be forced to insult him."

Two minutes later he was standing by their table. He was seventy-two and still considered himself a player. "Surely it's not true that two beautiful young women like you do not drink champagne?" he demanded.

"Hello," Natalie said, putting on a sugary sexy voice. "I'm a stripper at the Body Shop on Sunset. Be there at ten tonight. Fifty bucks and I'll perform a special lap dance just for *you!*" The man took a step back. "See you later," Natalie said, barely able to contain her laughter. The would-be player hurriedly returned to the bar. "Guess he doesn't watch TV," Natalie deadpanned.

"I like your line," Madison mused. "Maybe *I* should use it sometime."

"Ha!" Natalie said. "Who'd believe *you* were a

stripper? But me, black and pretty—why the hell not?"

"Oh, God! Don't start getting into racial stereotypes. You drove me insane with that crap in college."

"I'm simply saying it the way it is," Natalie said stubbornly. *"You're* a beautiful *white* woman. *I'm* a good-looking *black* woman. Guys *respect* you. They look at me and think—she's black, therefore she's easy."

"You're full of it."

"I live in this world," Natalie said, her voice rising. "I *know* I'm talking truth."

"What do you imagine *I* do—reside in a fairy-tale tower?"

"You're not black. *You* don't get it."

"I can't believe we're having this conversation again."

"Anyway," Natalie said. "I'm *glad* you're no longer with David, 'cause if he could run out on you, then he wasn't worth shit."

"The same goes for Denzl."

"What we *should* do is concentrate on our careers and become media moguls. You can *own* your magazine, and *I'll* be the first black Barbara Walters. How's that for a deal?"

"You got it going, girl."

"I love it when you try to talk black," Natalie said, giggling.

"What do you mean?"

"You're too uptight to get into jive talk."

"*Me*. Uptight?"

"You gotta loosen up—get yourself some attitude."

"What *kind* of attitude?"

"Like this, girl," Natalie said, high-fiving her. "Like this."

And they both broke into fits of raucous laughter.

chapter 11

KRISTIN WAS PUTTING the finishing touches to her appearance when the phone rang. She reached for it. "Hello?"

"A change of plan," Darlene said, all business. "Tomorrow, not tonight."

"You mean Mister X is canceling?"

"Not exactly canceling, merely rescheduling."

"Oh," Kristin said, relieved and yet disappointed because she had wanted the money.

"Tomorrow. Same time, same place," Darlene said. "Which won't interfere with your lunch. You'll have plenty of time to rest up between appointments."

"Thanks so much," Kristin drawled sarcastically.

"I know you don't like seeing Mister X," Darlene continued. "But what's not to like? He doesn't touch you, and he pays more than any other client."

"That's what's so weird," Kristin said. "I'm telling you, Darlene—there's something strange about him."

"Oh, *please,*" Darlene said, dismissing her fears as if they didn't matter. "Guys with fetishes—what's so unusual?"

Kristin put down the phone feeling depressed. She'd wanted to get it over with and done with. She'd psyched herself up for another kinky encounter; now she faced a long evening ahead with nothing planned.

For a moment her mind wandered over the events of the day, and she thought about Jake, the photographer with the tie problem. He had no idea who she was or what she did. "I'd really love to take your picture sometime," he'd said. So why not? It certainly wasn't going to lead to anything. Why couldn't she do something *she* might enjoy for a change?

On impulse she picked up the phone and obtained the number of the Sunset Marquis.

When the hotel operator answered, she realized she had no idea what his surname was. "Uh . . . do you have a Jake staying there?" she said. "He's a photographer. I seem to have forgotten his last name."

"Let me check that out for you," said the operator obligingly, and a few moments later she was put through to his room.

He answered immediately. "Bunny?" he said.

"Not Bunny," she replied, wondering who Bunny was.

"Hey—*Kristin,*" he said, sounding pleased to hear from her. "What a *nice* surprise. Why are you calling?"

Why *was* she calling? "Uh . . . I lied," she said.

"You did?"

"I . . . I don't have a fiancé. What I *do* have is a very jealous husband."

"And you couldn't wait to tell me."

"We're separated."

"That's encouraging."

A long pause, during which neither of them spoke. Kristin finally broke the silence, surprising herself. "Are you free for dinner tonight?"

"Me?" he said, obviously stalling for time.

"No. Mel Gibson," she said shortly, sorry she'd asked.

"Uh . . . are you saying that you *can* have dinner with me?"

"That's exactly what I'm saying."

"What time would you like me to pick you up?"

"I'll meet you," she said quickly, not wanting him to know where she lived.

"Okay," he said slowly. "And where will that be?"

Her mind wouldn't function. She didn't want to meet him where there might be people who knew her. "I'll . . . I'll come to your hotel," she said.

Wrong! Now he would think she was easy. Ha! If he only knew *how* easy. Expensive, but easy all the same.

"If that's what makes you happy," he said. "What time shall I expect you?"

It was so long since she'd gone on a legitimate date that she had no idea what to suggest. "How about seven-thirty?" she said, thinking that would give her plenty of time to change out of her white pristine outfit and get into something more suitable.

"You got it," he said.

"You're sure you can do this?" she asked, half hoping he'd tell her he was busy.

"Would I say yes if I couldn't?"

"No . . ."

"What's your number in case I need to reach you?"

"I'm not at home," she lied, quickly putting down the phone so she wouldn't have to answer his question. Then she was mad at herself. *What are you doing?* she thought. *Why are you going out on a stupid date with a stupid guy that you don't even know?*

Because I'm entitled to have some fun sometime, aren't I? I'm entitled to behave like a real human being.

No, you're not. You chose to be a whore. Stick to what you know.

She turned up at his hotel on time—punctuality was a prerequisite of the perfect call girl. He was waiting in the lobby, still looking somewhat rumpled in his brown leather jacket and longish hair. She'd changed outfits ten times, finally settling on a simple black dress and a couple of pieces of good jewelry—given to her by an Arab arms dealer. As soon as she saw him she realized she was too dressed up.

"Hey," he said, walking toward her. "This is a really nice surprise."

"It is?" she answered.

"You bet," he said, smiling. She smiled back. "Where do you want to go?" he asked.

"Uh . . . wherever *you* want to go."

"I'm the new boy in town."

She considered the possibilities. Clients took her to all the expensive clubs and restaurants. A few of the maître d's knew her and what she did. "How about . . . Hamburger Hamlet?" she said, thinking fast.

"You look too pretty to hang out at a hamburger joint."

"Don't be silly," she said. "I love hamburgers."

"If that's what you'd like."

I like you, a little voice screamed in her head. *I like you because you're normal, because you're not going to pay me. Because you don't know what I do, or anything about me. I like you because you like me just for who I am.*

"My car or yours?" he said, walking her outside the hotel. "Yours is probably better because all I've got is a beat-up old truck, which, I can assure you, has definitely seen better days."

"Let's take yours," she said, thinking that tonight she wanted to feel like an ordinary girl out on an ordinary date. Nothing wrong with that.

"So," he said, as they got into his truck. "What made you change your mind?"

"About what?"

"About going out with me?"

"You never asked."

"'Cause when you got on that escalator today, you had no intention of ever seeing me again."

"Why do you say that?"

"I can read people."

"See how wrong you were."

"I'm glad."

They went to the Hamburger Hamlet on Doheny and sat in a cozy booth, side by side. Kristin ordered a double cheeseburger and an extra thick chocolate milkshake. She felt like she was back in high school and out on a date.

Jake had plenty to say. He talked about photography and the people he'd met and worked with. He told her about the six months he'd lived in New York and how he'd hated it. She learned that although he was an award-winning photographer with several prestigious exhibitions behind him, he did not take himself too seriously. He made her laugh about his aging father and his father's future bride. She loved listening to him. He was interesting, funny, self-deprecating and undeniably attractive.

"I haven't done this in years," she said, enjoying every decadent minute as she sipped the thick chocolate shake through a straw.

"Done what?"

"Pigged out."

"How come?"

She hesitated for a moment. "My, uh, husband doesn't frequent places like this."

"Let me take a guess," Jake said, peering at her intently. "Your husband is very rich and much older than you—correct?"

She nodded. *Yes, Jake. They're all older than me, and they're all rich and lecherous and disgustingly kinky.* "That's right," she murmured.

"You're too beautiful to stay in an unhappy marriage," he said, his brown eyes genuinely concerned. "You're in a trap, you should get out while you can."

"I know," she said, thinking that marriage was a metaphor for the life she really led.

"Do you have a good lawyer?"

"The best," she answered, summoning up a mental picture of suave Binden Masters, the man who represented all of Darlene's girls.

"Then you should tell him you want out."

"I . . . I plan to," she said, studying his lips, wondering what it would be like to kiss him—a real kiss, not a paid-for performance.

He caught her looking and began asking more questions. She immediately became evasive, not wishing to tell him anything. After a while he realized he was being stonewalled and backed off, calling for the check.

"Come on," he said, getting up. "I'd better take

you back to your car. It's been a tough day, and it's rapidly catching up with me."

A tough day? Choosing ties? What was *his* problem?

"Fine," she murmured, pretending to be totally unconcerned. "I'm tired, too."

This was unbelievable. He was in line to get something for free that she usually charged exorbitantly for, and he was *tired!* Or maybe he was meeting Bunny—whoever *she* might be.

Whatever. She didn't care.

Next time she'd think twice before trying to experience life like a normal person.

chapter 12

THE RUNNING TRACK AT UCLA was not crowded. Madison was surprised; she'd expected it to be packed. But then, of course, it was quite early. She'd gotten there just before seven and began jogging in place because it was chilly. She looked around to see if she could spot Cole and his client. No sight of them yet.

Cole had suggested that she wear something hot, but she was not into luring Max with her supposed sex appeal—she was sure he had all the actresses and models he could handle. So she'd put on a warm tracksuit, stuffing her long black hair under a red baseball cap.

She was busy doing leg stretches when Cole and Max finally came into view. Cole was certainly an impressive-looking hunk of male flesh. Max Steele paled in comparison, although he was still attractive in a flashy, up-front Hollywood mogul way.

"Hey, Madison—" Cole said, waving at her. "What're *you* doin' here?"

"What does it look like I'm doing?" she replied, trying not to shiver. "Jogging of course. You think us New Yorkers never get out on the track?"

"Didn't realize you were into it," Cole said, playing his part well.

"Oh, yes," she lied. Truth was she wasn't into physical activities at all, and had to force herself to go to the gym twice a week.

Max was busy checking her out. "Hello," he said, extending his hand. "Max Steele."

"*You're* Max Steele?" Madison said, feigning surprise. "This is such a coincidence."

"How's that?"

"Max Steele of the International Artists Agency?"

"Unless there's another Max Steele lurking around that I don't know about."

"I'm Madison Castelli. I write for *Manhattan Style*. I'm in L.A. to do a piece on your agency."

"Then how come I don't know about you?" Max said, still checking her out and liking what he saw.

"Because I'm supposed to be meeting with Freddie Leon tomorrow. I was told that *he* was the man to talk to."

"Oh, you were told that, were you?" Max said, obviously irritated. "Were you also told that Freddie and I happen to be partners?"

"I understand Freddie Leon runs the agency, but of course I've heard of you."

"That's nice," Max said sarcastically. "Truth is you'll be hearing a lot more about me."

"I will?"

"Bet your pretty ass." She frowned. He didn't appear to notice. "Want to jog with us?" he asked.

"I'd love to." Second lie of the day.

They started out slowly, Cole moving to the front while Madison stayed behind next to Max. "How did you get started in the agency business?" she asked.

He began to talk, telling her all about the mail room at William Morris, and how he and Freddie had made a daring escape and started I.A.A. together.

Within minutes she was out of breath. "You know what?" she gasped. "I haven't done this in a while. Can we go somewhere for breakfast when you're through?"

"I haven't even seen your credentials," Max said, squinting at her. "Maybe I shouldn't be talking to you."

"My credentials?" she said, pretending to be offended. "I write the Profile on Power piece every month. Call my editor if you want. Victor Simons. I'm sure he'll be happy to fill you in."

"I don't have to," Max said. "On account of the

fact I've decided to trust you. But I *would* like to see some pieces you've written."

"I'll have New York E-mail you my interviews with Magic Johnson, John Kennedy, Jr., Henry Kissinger. Oh yes, and there's an interesting piece I did with Castro when I visited Cuba."

"Okay, okay, I'm impressed," Max said, laughing. "You're too attractive to be that serious."

"And you're too smart to come out with tired old lines."

"Did you ever consider a modeling career?"

"Did *you?*"

He laughed again and turned to Cole. "How do you know this lady?"

"She went to college with my sister."

"What do you say," Madison interrupted. "Can we meet for breakfast when you're through jogging?"

Max nodded, sliding a small cell phone from his jogging pants pocket. "Anna," he said into the phone. "Cancel my nine-o'clock breakfast, and book me a table for two at the Peninsula."

Madison grinned. "I guess that's a yes."

Breakfast with Max went well. He regaled her with stories of all the people he'd discovered whom he claimed he'd then made into enormous stars. Madison listened intently. It was difficult eliciting information about Freddie Leon because all Max really wanted to do was talk about himself and his achievements. She did manage to get some choice quotes; Max was hardly modest.

She knew she was not being up front with him regarding the interview, but she sensed that if he knew the piece was about Freddie Leon, he'd clam up. It was quite clear that Max's only interest was himself.

On their way out he offered to supply her with photographs and also suggested that later in the week she should come up to his office and they'd continue their conversation.

"There's something else," he said, as they stood outside the hotel waiting for valet parking to bring their cars.

"What's that?" she asked.

"I shouldn't be telling you this," he said. "It's strictly confidential, and completely off the record."

"I'm intrigued."

"In the next few weeks I'll be making an announcement that'll blow everyone away."

"How interesting. If I promise not to write it until you give me a green light, can you tell me what it is?"

Max shuffled his feet—quite large in fashionable silver and gray Nikes—then he looked around as though someone might be listening over his shoulder. "I . . . I can't say anything right now."

"Well . . . you know where to reach me. And yes—I'd love to come by your office sometime."

"When are you seeing Freddie?"

"It's being set up right now."

"You want me to put in a word for you?"

"That would be nice."

"Only remember—you need a star for this piece, and baby, you're *lookin'* at him."

"Right," she murmured, not appreciating the "baby" one little bit.

"Good." And he got into his shiny red Maserati and drove off.

chapter 13

"**D**UNNO WHAT YOU DID,
but I gotta say it—you're the freakin' best!"

"Thanks, Sam," Freddie replied, cursing his luck
for running into the small-time personal manager
in the parking area of his building. The very sight
of the short, bearded man aggravated him. "Who
are you here to see?"

"You, of course," replied Sam, tugging on his
graying beard as he followed Freddie to his private
elevator.

"I wasn't aware that we had an appointment,"
Freddie said, knowing full well they didn't.

"We don't," Sam said. "Took a chance you'd be
free for a minute or two."

"I have a very busy morning, Sam," Freddie

said, stepping into his elevator. "You'd best make an appointment with my assistant."

"Who needs appointments?" Sam said, trailing him into the elevator. "I can say what I have to on the way up."

No escape, Freddie thought sourly. "What's on your mind, Sam?"

"It's like this," Sam announced, quite full of himself. "I'm here t' do you a favor, but if you don't have time to hear what I havta say . . ."

Freddie swallowed his annoyance. "Go ahead," he said shortly.

"I'm givin' you the lowdown," Sam said, speaking out of the side of his mouth like a character in a Damon Runyon movie. "Max Steele's plannin' on takin' a powder an' sellin' his share of I.A.A. to the highest bidder. This I got from someone real close to the source."

Freddie had learned in life to always listen, never volunteer information. So instead of saying, "I already know," he was quiet for a moment. Then he said, "Tell me what you have."

"Well," Sam said, puffed up with his own importance. "Your partner's been havin' closed-door meetings with Billy Cornelius regarding Orpheus Studios. An' from what my *very reliable* source tells me, Billy's plannin' on bringin' in your Maxie boy as head of production, with an eye to him taking over the whole shebang when Billy dumps Ariel Shore."

"Interesting," Freddie said, his poker face giving nothing away.

"Word on the street is that these negotiations are C.I.A. secret," Sam said, digging at his teeth with a dirty fingernail. "So I gotta say to myself I'd better alert Freddie—just in case he don't know."

Freddie gave Sam a long, cold look. "Do you think anything happens in this town that I'm *not* aware of? Do you honestly think that?"

Sam backed down. "Just makin' sure," he said, fidgeting nervously, because being in Freddie Leon's company was enough to give anyone a case of the hives.

"I appreciate the information," Freddie said evenly.

"An' I 'preciate you gettin' that bitch to sign her contract," Sam grumbled. "What a cooze!"

Freddie froze him with a look. "Don't *ever* call Lucinda names," he said, as the elevator stopped at his private floor. "She's your client, and you should show her nothing but respect. She's made you a lot of money over the years. You'd be wise to remember that."

"I . . . I kiss her goddamn ass," the little man blustered, turning red in the face.

Freddie gave him another long, cold look, strode past Ria's desk, entered his private office and slammed the door. Sam Lowski was the dregs; if he hadn't latched on to Lucinda early in her career, he'd be nowhere now. As it was, without her as a client, he was less than nothing, and Freddie abhorred having to deal with scum. But his information was right on the money—confirming what Freddie already knew.

Ariel Shore was the studio head at Orpheus, and a good friend of Freddie's. He'd observed her swift rise to power and enjoyed her success, because she was a smart woman and knew how to play the game better than most men. Like him she was a killer in business with a charming manner and plenty of style.

Billy Cornelius was another matter. Billy, a tall, red-faced, seventy-two-year-old billionaire, didn't just own Orpheus, he owned a whole slew of entertainment companies and business corporations. A media king—he was also a son of a bitch who'd stab you in the back soon as look at you.

Over the last year Max Steele had formed an alliance with Billy. An unlikely duo, but Freddie had never complained, because having Billy Cornelius on the side of I.A.A. was a definite plus.

Ria buzzed him. "Your wife's on the line."

He picked up the phone. "Yes," he said into the receiver.

"I was wondering," Diana said tentatively. "Would you like me to fax you the seating plan for tonight?"

Damn! He'd forgotten. They were having another one of Diana's boring little dinner parties. "Who's coming?" he said shortly.

"The people you approved last week," Diana answered, sounding uptight. "Remember? We went over the list together."

"Fax me the list and seating. I'll check it."

"I could do a good job if you'd let me," Diana ventured.

"No, Diana, leave it to me," he replied.

"Fine." And she put the phone down hard.

Freddie sat behind his desk quietly for a moment, wondering why he was always so mean to his wife. He knew he treated her in a cold, uncaring fashion, and yet he couldn't help himself. It was as if he resented the fact they were married. Poor Diana. In public she was the perfect wife—never let him down, was always by his side, well dressed, cultured. At home she was available in the bedroom whenever he was in the mood—which wasn't often, because he'd lost interest in sex with his wife. They'd been married for over ten years, and there was no more of that sexual passion he'd felt in the first throes of their relationship. Also, she was the mother of his children; therefore, he could no longer regard her as a sexual object. Besides, sex drained a man's energy, and he needed every ounce of energy for his work. Thank God she had her charity functions and the children to keep her busy.

He considered the fact that news of Max Steele's upcoming defection was out on the street. If Sam Lowski knew, everybody must. Freddie decided the time had come to do something about it. Yes, he would deal with Max as only he knew how.

Ria knocked and entered his office carrying two faxes from Diana, which she handed to him. The guest list and the seating placement. He studied the guest list first. Max Steele was on it; he was bringing Inga Cruelle. Vaguely, Freddie remembered Max telling him about the gorgeous supermodel. "Most fuckable piece of ass you've ever seen" had been Max's description. "We gotta put her in something."

Yes, we must, Freddie thought. *We'll put her in the middle of a face-to-face confrontation between you and me, Max. Because if you think you're going to walk without telling me, you have another think coming.*

Freddie continued to study the list. Lucinda and her new boyfriend, Dmitri. That should be interesting. Kevin Page and his current girlfriend, Angela Musconni—nothing like new young talent to give an evening heat. The other guests were a billionaire businessman and his wife, a New York financier and his L.A. mistress, and the head of one of the TV networks. Not a bad mix.

Freddie put down the list. An invitation to the Leons' was a much-sought-after prize—he had to give Diana points for creating evenings that everyone fought to be invited to.

He buzzed Ria. "Get me Ariel Shore," he said abruptly. "And if she's not at the studio—find her. I need to speak to her immediately."

chapter 14

KRISTIN HAD A REGULAR, once-a-month client who liked to lunch with her before watching her perform with a girl of his choice. Over lunch he made her regale him with tales about her previous month's customers, and he in turn fed her unbelievable dish about Hollywood stars. Not that she was interested—she couldn't care less about who was doing what to whom. As a professional she kept her mouth shut and did her job to the best of her ability. Ratting on a john was a no-no.

So instead of revealing the truth, she made up tales of outrageous sexual goings-on, while her client listened with gleaming eyes and a satisfied smile.

Usually after her session with this particular

client, she visited her sister in the nursing home just outside Palm Springs where—as long as Kristin could afford to pay the bills—Cherie resided permanently. Today she couldn't go because Mister X had rescheduled. Damn Mister X! Everything about him made her skin crawl. His disguise, his kinky demands. He was sinister, maybe even dangerous.

She dressed for lunch in a simple, pale beige Armani suit. Underneath the jacket she wore a plunging cream-color blouse and no bra so that the darkness of her nipples showed through the flimsy fabric. Her client enjoyed having other men in the restaurant look and lust. Little did he know that several of them were also clients of hers who knew exactly who she was and what she did.

He liked to lunch at Morton's, where he had a regular table. Kristin arrived first and sat down, wondering, as she always did, what this particular guy's trip was. He was powerful, not unattractive, with a manic if somewhat over-the-top personality—he could probably take his pick of most of the young actresses and models in Hollywood, and yet, he chose to have lunch with her once a month, and then pay for sex. Not so strange really. If she was a date he'd be forced to make small talk, send flowers, buy gifts, build up to the final moment. With her it was a sure thing, he'd pay her and she'd go home. No strings. A simple business deal.

Plus she had no objections to performing with another girl. Why would she? It was her profession. She knew that a lot of the women who did what she did were lesbians, so turned off by men and the way they treated women that they'd switched leagues. Although Kristin knew how to make all the right moves, she had no inclination in that direction.

She watched her client as he made his entrance, smiling and joking with several people as he passed by their tables. He was a nice enough guy, she didn't mind their monthly meetings. It was seeing Mister X later that was freaking her out.

"Hi, Max," she said, as he sat down at the table.

"Hi, doll," Max Steele replied, summoning the waiter and ordering an iced tea. His mind was dodging this way and that. There was so much going on, and yet all he could think about was his date that night with Inga Cruelle. She was giving him a hard time and he liked it. Max considered the chase everything. Once he scored, he was out of there. Which is why he'd never married, and why he enjoyed meeting Kristin once a month. No demands, sensational sex, and the two-girls-together fantasy he'd dreamt about since first drooling over the centerfolds in *Playboy* at thirteen.

"How have you been, Max?" Kristin asked politely.

"Pretty damn good," he replied. "I'm in shape, business is zooming, it's all happenin', babe."

"Still single?" Kristin inquired, not really interested, but she knew he liked her to appear as if she cared.

He roared with laughter. "You know *me,* baby— one woman could never do it for me." He took a couple of healthy swigs of iced tea and leaned eagerly toward her. "So c'mon, honeysuckle, gimme the goods—what's been going on in hooker land?"

"Well," she said, toying with the glass of wine she'd prudently ordered, although she didn't usually drink on appointments. "There was this politician who came into town from Washington, someone *very* high up in the Senate."

Max leaned even closer; this was the kind of stuff he got a buzz from. If only he could get names out of her, but she was adamant about never revealing her clients' identities. In a way it was a good thing—it meant she'd never talk about him. "You wanna give me his name?" he asked, hopeful as ever.

An enigmatic smile. "You know I can't do that."

He ran a hand through his curly brown hair. "You're somethin' else, babe. How come you chose to be a hooker, not an actress or model?"

"You ask me that every time, Max."

"What's the answer?"

"I can *choose* who I sleep with." *Not true,* she thought. *If you can choose, why are you meeting Mister X, when you know he's a sick pervert?* "Models and actresses—they have to cater to people, they're worried about their next magazine cover, their next movie. Me—I never have to worry about the next client, they're lining up."

"You gonna name the politician?" Max asked eagerly, hungry for information.

Kristin shook her head. "You know I'm not."

"Okay, okay," Max said, giving up. "But you can

at least tell me what he got up to—or down to—depending on his trip."

"Well . . ." Kristin began, making up a fabulously erotic story that made Max's eyes bug.

Their ritual was always the same. An hour-long lunch, during which she fed him sexy stories which she swore were true, and some of which were. Then she'd follow his car to the Century Plaza Hotel, where he'd rented a penthouse suite. Another girl would be waiting, and after snorting a little coke, the three of them would go in the bedroom. Max would sit in a chair, watching and barking orders, while they did everything he requested. Sometimes he joined in. Sometimes he didn't. Then he would hand out cash and everybody would go home.

She'd repeated this scenario with Max Steele for almost a year now, and the order of events never varied.

Idly she wondered how he'd react if she told him the only reason she was doing this was to support her sister who lay in a coma in a nursing home. Would he offer money and help her to get out of the business? Or would he merely put an end to their monthly meetings because she made him feel guilty? It was difficult to know.

Max glanced at his gold Rolex watch. He'd almost canceled Kristin today, thinking he might save himself for the evening's activities. But then it had occurred to him that it might be better to indulge in some afternoon sex. That way he wouldn't be too anxious with Inga. He'd be in control, so if he *did* manage to get into her sexy little thong, he could give her the great lover treatment he was famous for. Sex with Kristin would keep his appetite at bay. She was very good at what she did.

He studied her face as she sipped her wine. She was quite a knockout, in a totally different way from Inga. Blond, fresh and pretty, the girl-next-door look with a body to die for.

Max had only been in love once, and that was with a girl in high school who'd treated him badly, humiliating him in front of his friends. He'd never forgotten her, never forgiven her either.

It was nice to be with a woman whom he controlled for an hour or so.

It was satisfying to be able to call every shot.

chapter 15

"**HI.**" SALLI T. ANSWERED
the door of her huge Pacific Palisades mansion
herself. She was barefoot, wearing a skimpy little
sundress that barely covered the top of her thighs.
What was most evident were her long skinny
brown legs, huge silicone boobs, white-blond hair
and an abundance of makeup. "It's *so* good to see
you," she said, full of enthusiasm. "Come on in."

Madison entered the vast mansion, where she
was immediately set upon by two small, fluffy
white dogs who jumped all over her ankles, sniffing
and barking.

"This is Muff and Snuff," Salli T. said, making
no attempt to call them off. "Aren't they adorable?
Bobby bought them for me on our wedding day. We

took them on our honeymoon, and they crapped all over the bedroom. Boy—was he *furious!* But you know what? Now he loves them as much as I do." She scooped up one of the barking dogs and nuzzled its furry little face into hers. "I'm so *happy* when I'm around animals. Do you have a pet?"

Madison shook her head. "It's not that easy when you live in a New York apartment."

"Tell you what," Salli T. said brightly. "If these two ever have puppies, I'll send you one. I read this thing once where it said you live ten years longer if you own a dog."

"Ten years longer than what?"

Salli T. squealed with laughter. "You're so *funnee!"*

Madison looked around. The front hall was all soft pile carpets and soaring mirrored walls. Directly facing her was a giant portrait of Salli T., bare-assed, lying facedown on a white sheepskin rug.

"That was from my first *Playboy* shoot," Salli said proudly. "I know it's kind of a trip to hang it in the front hall, but it sure gets a lot of attention!" She giggled. "Bobby *loves* it. He brings all his friends by—just to take a peek."

"I bet he does," Madison murmured.

An Asian man in tight orange pants and a white tank top appeared in the hall. "This is Froo," Salli said, waving in his direction. "Anything you want, all you gotta do is ask. He's fixing us lunch. And after, if you want a massage, he does that, too."

"No, thank you," Madison said quickly.

"You *sure?"* Salli said, leading her through the living room, outside to an Olympic-size, brilliant blue pool. "If you let him near your feet, it's totally orgasmic!"

Madison took in the view of the ocean, which shimmered like a glorious picture postcard.

"We can swim after lunch," Salli said. "It's *real* good for the boobs—keeps 'em up, if you know what I mean!"

"Didn't occur to me to bring my swimsuit," Madison said.

"That's okay, I'll lend you something."

The thought of her slim figure in one of Salli T.'s outrageous black rubber swimsuits brought a smile to Madison's lips.

"We're eating beside the pool," Salli said. *"Sooo* Hollywood. But, y'know, this is what I dreamed about when I was a little girl. I *wished* I'd get to live in a place like this. And my wish came true. Sometimes I have to pinch myself—isn't that crazy?"

"You know," Madison said, sensing that this was going to be a terrific piece. "That's exactly what I'd like to talk about. Your dreams, how you got here, the way the people you met on the way up treated you, the men in Hollywood, all of that stuff."

"Wow!" Salli giggled. "Usually people just wanna know how big my boobs are."

"Well, today," Madison said, "will certainly be different."

chapter 16

JUST AS KRISTIN HAD FIN-
ished dressing all in white for her meeting with
Mister X, her phone rang. To answer or not to
answer—that was the question. It might be Mister
X canceling again, or perhaps the nursing home
with news of Cherie. She couldn't allow herself the
luxury of *not* answering her phone, so she quickly
picked up.

"Is this the hamburger queen?" said a male
voice.

"Huh?"

"It's me, Jake. Am I catching you at a bad time?"

On impulse she'd given him her number, but
she'd never thought he'd call. In spite of herself she
felt a tiny buzz of excitement. "Well . . ." she said
hesitantly.

He sighed. "Guess I am."

"No, no . . ." she said quickly. "I can talk."

"I realize this is kind of late notice," Jake said, "but I'm on my way to my brother's house for a home-cooked meal. Can you come?"

No, Jake, I will be otherwise engaged with a disgusting perverted freak.

"I'd love to, only—"

"I know, I know," he said ruefully. "You've probably got guys lined up around the block."

What did he mean by *that?*

"Actually, I have a business appointment," she said stiffly.

"I was thinking," he said. "What with me doing all the talking last night, I never got around to asking what *you* do."

I'm a call girl, sweetheart. Extremely expensive. Very talented. So if you know what's good for you— stay away.

"I . . . uh . . . I'm a makeup artist," she lied. "I go to people's homes and give them a professional makeup."

"No kidding?"

"Yes. It's what I do."

"Hey," he said cheerfully. "In that case maybe I can hire you."

"Excuse me?" she said, frowning.

"Photographer. Makeup artist. We should work together."

One part of her wanted to keep talking, but sanity warned her to steer clear of all personal relationships. Getting involved could only lead to big trouble.

Then why did you give him your phone number?

How the hell should I know?

"Uh . . . I have to go," she said, aware that she sounded flustered. "I'm running late for my appointment."

"How about I give you my brother's address, and maybe you can drop by later when you're through?" A meaningful pause. "I'd very much like to see you again, Kristin."

And I'd like to see you, too, Jake.

"Okay," she said, reaching for a piece of paper and a pen.

She had no intention of going—but just in case she changed her mind . . .

On their way to Jimmy Sica's house in the Valley, Madison recounted her afternoon with Salli T. "I never thought I'd say this," she said. "But Salli's adorable. If I was a guy, I'd probably fall in love with her—silicone boobs and all."

"Oh, come *on,*" Natalie said disbelievingly, as she raced her car along the freeway. "Salli T. Turner is the definitive Hollywood cliché. All giant tits and candy-floss hair."

"She *plays* that role," Madison explained. "Which is why she's so successful. But I'm here to tell you that underneath all the dumb gloss and glitter lurks a very nice little kid who's enjoying every moment. Trust me—this woman had it tough getting to the top."

"Sure," Natalie said with a toss of her head. *"I* can tell you about tough."

"Don't be such a mean bitch."

"I'm *not* a bitch," Natalie objected indignantly. "I'm merely voicing the way *everyone* thinks about her."

"No, you're being judgmental. If you got to know her, I promise you—you'd really like her."

"Okay, okay, if you say so," Natalie said, barely missing a huge truck as she skimmed past. "And how about the cute husband? Did you get to meet him?"

"He's in Vegas," Madison said, making sure her seat belt was firmly buckled because Natalie's driving was a trip indeed. "He called ten times, and they had these lovey-dovey conversations. It was quite sweet. They certainly seem to be in love."

Natalie pulled a face. "Think I'm gonna throw up!"

"Will you stop being such a cynic."

"Thing *I'm* surprised at is you," Natalie chided, as she zoomed alongside a Ferrari. "I'd take a bet with you that their marriage will not make it to the end of the year."

"No, Natalie," Madison said, shaking her head. "You're wrong. What they have between them is genuine. Y'see, they both come from small towns, both arrived in L.A. determined to make it big. Now they've got everyone falling all over them to do anything they want, and they're loving it. I'm telling you, I like her a lot, and so would you if you got to know her."

Natalie was still unconvinced. *"Puleease,"* she said.

"She told me some great stories," Madison offered.

This got Natalie's attention. "Hmm . . ." she said, eyes gleaming. "Tell me every detail."

"No. You'll have to read about them in the magazine like everyone else."

"Oh, come *on,"* Natalie complained, almost rear-ending a white Toyota. "You wouldn't do that to me—your best friend."

Madison placed her hands on the dashboard. "Oh, yes, I would."

"Here's the deal," Natalie said, blithely changing lanes. *"You* give me all the juicy bits before the magazine hits the stands, and *I'll* do a whole program on it—y'know, give the mag a big plug so people'll be racing out to buy it."

"I hate to tell you this," Madison said, "but they race out anyway."

"Why can't you be like everyone else and get behind plugging something?" Natalie grumbled as she exited the freeway, cutting off a man in a sports car who gave her the finger.

"In my next life," Madison joked.

"You're no fun."

"Never said I was."

A few minutes later Natalie pulled her car to a shuddering stop in front of a modest country-style house on a quiet side street. "Okay, so I'd better fill you in on Jimmy Sica."

"What about him?" Madison asked, releasing her seat belt, relieved they'd arrived in one piece.

"He's incredibly handsome, with a lovely wife—picture displayed proudly on his desk." A succinct pause. "And . . . I think he's coming on to me."

Madison raised an eyebrow. "What do you mean, you *think* he's coming on to you? Either he is or he isn't."

"Well," Natalie said unsurely. "I *guess* he is, but somehow I can't believe it 'cause he's married to such a gorgeous woman."

"Oh, like you're *not* gorgeous. Is that your new trip—putting yourself down?"

"I'm not his type."

"Maybe it's not a *type* he's looking for. Maybe a fast blow job would do it for him."

"Get your mind out of the gutter, girl!"

Laughing, they both got out of the car.

"You know, you're awfully naïve, Nat," Madison said, as they walked toward the house. "Married men are all the same—none of them would say no to a little action on the side."

"*Now* who's sounding cynical."

"Well, it's the truth," Madison said defensively.

"Yeah, yeah, you and your truths."

"Listen, do what you want, but I'm here to tell you that I have absolutely no respect for married men who cheat."

"Get a life, girl. That's major unrealistic."

"I suppose so, especially when we have a president who does it all the time." She shook her head. "What in hell happened to moral values?"

Natalie shrugged as they reached the front door. "Moral values—what's that?"

"Wasn't it something we used to believe in when we were in college?" Madison said dryly. "Remember?"

"That was before all these tell-all books came out revealing every little detail."

Madison frowned. "I find it totally disheartening that every president from Kennedy on was running around the Oval Office with his dick in his hand and WD-forty on his zipper!"

Natalie giggled and pressed the doorbell. "A power hard-on! Tell me—please—where can I find one?"

Madison, sardonically: "Like I said—try the White House."

chapter 17

KRISTIN WAS EXCITED, and it wasn't at the thought of seeing Mister X again. As she sat behind the wheel of her car, driving toward her destination, she couldn't keep her mind off Jake. It was ridiculous really, because she was too smart to let anyone come between her and her goal of scoring enough money to get out of the call-girl business. And if she allowed herself to get involved, that's exactly what would happen.

Forget about him, her cold, calculating side warned her. *He's only another john who doesn't think he has to pay.*

And yet . . . he had a warmth and a laid-back sincerity, friendly eyes and a smile that melted her heart.

For the first time since she'd started in the business she actually felt a deep sexual longing. She *wanted* to sleep with him, she yearned to have long, leisurely unpaid-for sex, wake up in the morning to find herself safely enclosed in his strong arms.

Get real.

Why should I?

She pulled up at a stoplight and began drumming her fingers nervously on the steering wheel. Enough thoughts about Jake; she'd better get ready to deal with Mister X and his bound-to-be-kinky demands.

She'd dressed all in white, as instructed, including a short dress and white-framed Christian Dior sunglasses. Darlene had faxed her the address of the motel where she was to meet him, and she was to sit in her parked car outside cabin six until further notice.

A car pulled up next to her, and the male driver leered suggestively through the window. She pretended not to notice and drove quickly off.

The motel—way down Hollywood Boulevard—was a seedy, run-down dump. Automatically she checked that her car door was locked as she pulled into the dilapidated courtyard and drove up to cabin six.

A drunk ambled out of the shadows carrying a half-empty bottle of cheap Scotch. He winked at her, burping loudly as he lurched past her car.

Ten minutes passed. She tried to stay calm, thinking only of the four thousand dollars and how it would pay her sister's hospital bills for a while.

IF ONLY I DIDN'T HAVE TO DO THIS!

Ah, but you do.

A gloved hand knocked on her window. A man in a chauffeur's uniform all in black—his peaked cap pulled low over his forehead—opaque wraparound shades completely covering his eyes.

Was it Mister X?

She couldn't tell.

"Leave your car here and come with me," he said in a muffled voice.

She took a deep breath and got out of her car, locking it behind her.

"Over here," the chauffeur muttered, leading her toward a dark-colored limo parked curbside.

He opened the rear door and she obediently climbed inside. He moved to the front of the car and slid behind the wheel.

"Where are we going?" she asked, a certain numbness taking over her mind.

"Mister X requires you to put on a blindfold," the chauffeur said, without turning around. "You will find it on the seat beside you."

She groped on the plush leather seat, found the blindfold and placed it over her eyes.

Four thousand dollars. Cash. It didn't matter. This was the last time she'd do business with Mister X.

chapter 18

DIANA LEON GREETED her husband at the front door of their Bel Air mansion. "You're late," she said crossly.

"Didn't realize I was on a time clock," Freddie said, entering the house, which was now full of caterers preparing for their dinner party.

"How can you do this to me?" she said, glaring at him.

"Do what?" he said, distracted and out of breath.

"Invite an extra two guests."

"You can fit 'em in," he said, hurriedly heading for the stairs.

"No, I can't," Diana said, angrily following him.

"Our dining table accommodates sixteen people, now you've added two more."

"So we'll squeeze a little. No big deal."

"Why didn't you put them on our original list?"

"Diana," he said irritably. "Do I tell you how to run the house?"

"No."

"Then don't tell me how to run my business," he snapped. "It's extremely important that Ariel is here tonight."

"*And* her husband, whom you can't stand," Diana pointed out, her voice tart.

"Sometimes you have to put up with the guy behind the woman, or *under* the woman, as the case may be."

"Ariel was here last month," Diana said, folding her arms.

"So now we're having her again."

Diana followed him into the bedroom. "Why did you leave it until the last minute?"

"Oh, for God's sake," he snapped, entering his private bathroom. "I have to take a shower. Leave me alone." And with that he slammed the door in her face.

Once rid of Diana, he stood in front of his marble vanity and stared blankly into his shaving mirror. Moments passed before he cleared his mind and began thinking coherently. He still couldn't believe that Max would be stupid enough to attempt to sell out his half of I.A.A. without consulting him first. Surely he had some idea of what it would be like to have Freddie Leon as an enemy?

No, Max Steele probably didn't, because Max thought with his dick most of the time—useful when dealing with female clients—but as any fool knew, the brain has more staying power than the dick any day. The brain is *always* hard.

"Hello, ladies," Jimmy Sica said, throwing open the front door of his house and ushering them inside.

"Hi," Madison replied, as they entered the comfortable house. Natalie was right, Jimmy Sica was incredibly handsome in an *I'm-a-TV-anchorman-with-a-sensational-smile* way.

"Nice to *meet* you," Jimmy said, squeezing her hand a tad too tightly as a chocolate-box-pretty blonde appeared behind him. "And this is my wife, Bunny," he added, putting his arm around Bunny's narrow waist.

"Bunny?" Madison questioned.

"I *know*," Bunny said, with a wide smile that matched her husband's. "It's *such* a silly name, everyone says so. I was nicknamed Bunny as a little girl, and it kind of stuck. I collected bunny rabbits, still do, only Jimmy makes me hide them in a closet."

"Now, now," Jimmy said, patting his wife on the ass. "Mustn't go giving away all our secrets. Madison's likely to write about them. She's a big-time writer from New York."

"I *know*," Bunny said, wriggling away from him.

"You already told me, Jimmy pie." She dazzled Madison with a big smile, revealing perfect white Chiclet teeth. "Welcome to our home, Madison. We're *so* excited to meet you. I hope we can all become good friends."

Oh God, Madison thought. *Why did I agree to do this? I'm perfectly happy alone. I could be writing my piece on Salli. I don't need to be with people. Especially these people.*

Natalie had gone straight over to the bar, plopping herself down on a velvet-covered bar stool.

"What'll you have?" Jimmy said, running over and deftly placing himself behind it.

"Isn't it margarita time?" Natalie replied, flirting in spite of herself. "Can you make one?"

"Can *I* make one?" Jimmy said, as if it was the most ridiculous thing he'd ever heard. *"I* can make anything I put my mind to." He gave her a look that underlined his double entendre.

Natalie quickly glanced around to see if Madison noticed, but Bunny was busy showing her a painting they'd recently bought of two rabbits being chased by a ferocious-looking fox. "The thing I like about this painting," Bunny explained to Madison in a serious voice, "is that the wicked old fox hasn't caught them yet. Isn't that something?"

"Uh-huh," Madison agreed, stifling a yawn.

A toilet flushed somewhere in the distance, then an exceptionally big, black man ambled into the room.

"Say hello to my college buddy, Luther," Jimmy said, steering him in the direction of Natalie.

Luther towered over her. "Luther used to play for the Chicago Bears," Jimmy offered. "That is, until he got his shoulder busted."

"Wow!" Natalie said, thinking that this was one big handsome hunk of a guy. "I guess you're okay now, huh?"

"Still alive, sister," Luther said, with a huge grin. "Got me a nice little electrical business. Better than gettin' the crap kicked outta me every weekend—'scuse my language. Oh, yeah, Jimmy tells me you're on TV with him."

"No," Natalie said. "Jimmy's on TV with me." And she smiled sweetly, realizing that if they ever had sex, she'd probably be crushed to death.

"Kevin, dear," Lucinda gushed, balancing a martini in one hand and a caviar-loaded toast point in the other. "I'm *thrilled* we're doing a project together. I've seen every one of your movies—three in eighteen months. Poor overworked boy—you must be *exhausted.*"

Kevin straightened up from a terminal slouch. "Thanks," he muttered, considering that a word with his agent might not be a bad thing. Now that he'd seen Lucinda Bennett in the flesh he realized she was too *old* for the part, she'd make him look ridiculous.

"Hey—Freddie," he said, veering in the super-agent's direction. "We gotta talk."

"Later," Freddie said, dismissing him with a wave of his hand. Ariel was at the door, and he needed to speak to her before Max put in an appearance.

Meanwhile, Max was pacing around his penthouse apartment in a fury, having just hung up on Inga. "I will be late, Max," she'd said, in her precise Swedish accent. "Go to the dinner and I will try to join you."

Try to join him. Was she totally nuts? Tonight was her big night, an opportunity to meet important people in the industry, and the silly Swedish blonde was blowing it. "Why?" he'd demanded. "What are you doing?"

"It's private," she'd answered curtly.

Bitch! Bitch! Bitch! Just who exactly did she think she was?

"You'd better make it, Inga," he'd said, endeavoring to remain calm. "If you want to be in movies, you'd better make it soon."

"We'll see," she'd said, infuriating him even more with her casual tone.

Now he would have to walk in alone. Shit! If Max Steele got stood up, it would be all over town by noon tomorrow. *Shit!*

chapter 19

JIMMY SICA WAS RUNNING around playing the perfect host, fixing margaritas, making small talk, flashing his unbelievable smile. While Bunny was busy showing pictures of their kids to the next-door neighbors, who'd dropped by for a drink, an extremely amiable Chinese couple whose grasp of the English language was somewhat elusive.

Madison could see that Natalie was getting along fine with Luther. *I wish I was at home, writing,* she thought for the twentieth time. *What am I doing here? This is not my kind of evening. I have enough casual friends in New York—no need to make new ones. And kiddie talk is not for me.*

She decided that after dinner she'd ask Natalie if she could borrow her car and leave. Luther would probably be only too delighted to drive Natalie home.

"And *this* is a photo of Blackie," Bunny announced proudly. "Blackie was my precious itsy bitsy black poodle who passed away last year." Her lower lip quivered. "I'm *still* grieving."

"Another margarita?" Jimmy suggested. "We're waiting for my brother, he's always late."

"Okay," Madison said, trailing him back to the bar.

"First trip to L.A.?" Jimmy asked, taking her empty glass.

"I've been here several times before."

"I guess you must do a lot of traveling," he said, turning on the blender.

Madison watched the frothy liquid as it spun around in its glass cage. "Natalie tells me you recently moved here from Denver," she remarked.

"Six months ago," he said, refilling her glass and handing it back to her. He paused, giving her a long, lingering look. "You know, Madison, I'm sure you've been told this many times."

"What?"

He flashed his handsome-anchorman smile, favoring her with another intimate look. "You're a powerfully attractive woman. In fact, you remind me of my first real love."

Oh, get a life, Jimmy Sica. What a tired old line. You'll be telling me your wife doesn't understand you next.

"Thanks," she murmured, ever polite. "You're not so bad yourself."

That shut him up for a moment.

Bunny ran over. "Where's—" she began.

But before she could finish her sentence, Jimmy's brother walked in. "I'm here," he said with a crooked grin, thrusting a bunch of flowers at her. "Late as usual."

"Thank *goodness!*" Bunny exclaimed, giving him a big hug and a squeeze. "We'd almost given up on you."

"Hey—" he said, still grinning. *"Never* give up on me, you know I always make it in the end."

Madison turned around to check out the new arrival. He was a rumpled version of the perfect TV anchor, only much sexier, with laughing brown eyes and longish brown hair.

"Meet my deadbeat brother, the photographer," Jimmy said with a twist of genuine affection. "Jake, say hello to Madison. You two should have a lot in common—Madison's a big-deal journalist."

"Yeah?" Jake said, giving her a firm handshake. "Big-deal, huh?"

"Not so big," Madison replied lightly, deciding that maybe tonight wasn't going to be such a dead loss after all. Jake had the look. And perhaps a quick fling with no responsibility was exactly what she needed.

"Who do you work for?" he asked.

"Manhattan Style."

"Very nice."

"It pays the rent."

"I bet it does."

"And you?" she asked.

"Mostly freelance."

"Really?"

"It pays the rent."

They smiled at each other, and then Natalie bounded over, giving Madison a not-so-subtle wink.

Jimmy put his arm around his brother's shoulders and walked him across the room. "You see how good I am to you," he said in a low voice. "Not one, but *two* beauties. Take your pick, although personally I'd go for the journalist—she's got that icy hot thing going. Very sexy."

"Spoken like a true married man," Jake said, rolling his eyes.

"Don't tell me you're *not* interested?"

"I met somebody."

"Who?"

"Just a girl. Nice. Pretty. Perfect."

"Oh, *shit,*" Jimmy said, bursting out laughing. "You're not in love for chrissake?"

"No . . ." Jake said, hesitating for only a moment. "It's just that there's something special about her—something I can't put into words. Hey—you'll soon see for yourself. I asked her over later."

"Can't wait."

"And *please,* don't hit on her," Jake warned.

Now it was Jimmy's turn to grin. "Like you said, I'm a married man, bro."

"Yeah, *right.*"

And together they returned to the bar.

Epilogue

THE BLONDE FELL WITH A sickening thud—the razor-sharp hunting knife cutting through her carotid artery as easy as slicing butter. Blood pumped from her like oil gushing from an open well.

The blonde attempted to scream, her eyes open wide with the fear and knowledge of what was to come next. But when she opened her mouth, blood gurgled out, spilling down her body and soaking her clothes.

Then her assassin struck again—the lethal knife viciously stabbing her breasts.

Once.

Twice.

Three times.

She sighed. A horrible death rattle of a sigh.

And within seconds she was dead.

TO BE CONTINUED . . .

**POCKET BOOKS
PROUDLY PRESENTS**

OBSESSION

BY JACKIE COLLINS

**Coming soon in paperback
from
Pocket Books**

**Turn the page for a preview of
Obsession. . . .**

Ariel Shore was a statuesque redhead in her late forties with an abundance of charm and a deceptively bland manner. Beneath the wide and welcoming smile lurked an astute woman who knew the movie business inside out—a woman who could sweet-talk like nobody else and then, if she felt like it, blow a deal right out the window without a second thought.

Ariel had started her illustrious career in advertising, moved on to marketing, produced a couple of low-budget films, and then she'd caught the attention of Billy Cornelius, who'd championed her rise to head of his studio. Some said Ariel and Billy were lovers. Freddie didn't believe it for a minute; Ariel was way too smart to sleep with her boss. Besides, Billy's feisty little wife, Ethel, watched him like a bird-dog—ever since he'd nearly left her for a curvaceous starlet with big silicone enhanced lips and a talent for latching onto other women's husbands. Ethel had seen to it that the girl was run out of Hollywood—forcing her to seek employment (and other women's husbands) in Europe.

Ariel was career driven like Freddie—which is why the two of them got along so well. They usually managed to have lunch a couple of times a month where they exchanged information—a lunch they both enjoyed because they genuinely liked each other.

Freddie greeted her at the door of his house, hugging her close, whispering in her ear how glad he was she'd made it.

"This was very short notice, Freddie," she scolded. "Only for you."

"I know, Ariel. I appreciate it."

"So you should. You owe me, Freddie. And I *always* collect."

Look for

Obsession

**Wherever Books
Are Sold
Coming Soon
in Paperback from
Pocket Books**

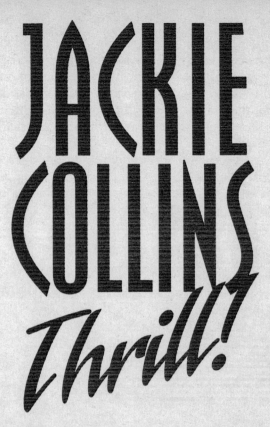

JACKIE COLLINS
Thrill!

AMERICA'S MOST SENSATIONAL NOVELIST

Now available in hardcover from Simon & Schuster

Coming soon in paperback from Pocket Books

 SIMON & SCHUSTER